COOKIE

COOKIE

Jan Adkins

1817

HARPER & ROW, PUBLISHERS, New York
Cambridge, Philadelphia, San Francisco, Washington
London, Mexico City, São Paulo, Singapore, Sydney

A HARPER NOVEL OF SUSPENSE

Grateful acknowledgment is made for permission to reprint the lines by Carl Sandburg from "Gone" in *Chicago Poems,* copyright 1916 by Holt, Rinehart & Winston, Inc.; renewed 1944 by Carl Sandburg. Reprinted by permission of Harcourt Brace Jovanovich.

FIRST EDITION
Copy editor: Marjorie Horvitz
Designer: Erich Hobbing

Library of Congress Cataloging-in-Publication Data

Adkins, Jan.
  Cookie.

  I. Title.
PS3551.D52C66   1988   813'.54   87-45826
ISBN 0-06-015867-0

88 89 90 91 92 HC 10 9 8 7 6 5 4 3 2 1

for Bug
Remember, love

Everybody loved Chick Lorimer in our town,
Far off, everybody loved her.
So we all love a wild girl
Keeping a hold on a dream she wants.

CARL SANDBURG, *"Gone"*

COOKIE

CHAPTER ONE

Cookie woke. She slapped the clock until it stopped its buzzing, and rolled out of the quilts and covers, naked, with a doom-filled groan.

She made a lot of noise in the bathroom, brushing her teeth and peeing, pausing to make a face at herself in the mirror. Damn. Late nights with Mr. Jack Daniel, bad mouth, thirty-five dollars lost to Bert and Willard; no cards. She dressed quickly: a silk chemise and two shirts, lace panties and Levi's. She spent more time fitting the wool socks than with anything else, getting them smooth and even, then the boots. Dan Posts, cowhide with veal tops, old friends. Done.

From a drawer beside the bed she took a Smith & Wesson .41 magnum, thumbed the release, and dropped the cylinder. Six chambers loaded. Long after her father had carried his .44 Single Action Army model, he kept an empty chamber under the hammer of his .38. Not Cookie.

Holding the revolver under her arm, she cinched up her belt and straightened her shirts in front of the mirror. Cookie Culler was not tall but looked taller than her five six. She was not slim, but carried flesh well. Her hips annoyed her. They were broad, muscular hips that did not swell at the thighs, that had no trace of fat or indolence, the hips of an athlete, a horsewoman. Yet it was like Cookie to take the remark of

1

the one lover who discounted them as the truth. To other men, those hips were the powerful center of a compelling woman whose sudden appearance caused a lull in taverns, stock shows, and restaurants. Indeed, if the disparaging remark had been made known around Cle Elum or Ellensburg, the lawyer who uttered it would have gone back to the District of Columbia drawling his Virginia vowels with difficulty. But that was Cookie: She had trouble believing anyone would lie, and she never took the easy road.

Around the mirror were framed pictures. Pete Culler in his sheriff's uniform; Pete with Cookie at ten holding her baby brother, Benjy. Pete beside the hanging carcass of a prize elk; Benjy and Pete (now with silver hair) trout fishing. Benjy's army photo, very serious and dedicated; Cookie at twenty-two with her arm around her twelve-year-old Benjy, protective, motherly. No pictures of a mother. One small black-rimmed frame with Pete's badge against black velvet. She looked at them buttoning her shirt, smiling at the boy and the man.

Across the hall, in the tack room, she took down a holster and snapped it over her belt on her left side, cross-draw, for the S & W. Out of the rifle rack she drew a Remington .35 pump-action rifle, a big brush gun; she fed five of the finger-sized cartridges into the magazine but didn't pump one up into the chamber. The rifle went into a saddle scabbard, and Cookie went into the living room.

The table was set for one, and tea was steaming in a mug. Toast under a napkin, a Mason jar of raspberry preserves, two eggs in eggcups, and a pottery bowl holding a yellow snowbutton floating in water. In the corner alcove, beside the fireplace, Nathan Lavenstein sat at a desk, surrounded by papers, ringed by a night's worth of fine pipe ash. He was pretending that he hadn't cooked the breakfast and folded the napkin like a little tent and picked the early spring flower. Or

2

he had completely forgotten that he had done these things. Fither was a possibility. Nathan was a physicist with a specialty in lasers. He forgot a lot, an aspect of his famous powers of concentration. Cookie thought he was Cute. Long and thin and smart and Cute.

She grinned and came up behind him, bent down and rubbed her chest across his wide, bony back. It felt good to her. If it didn't feel good to him he had even more concentration than expected. Still concentrating, he said, "Arr." He was a grumpy worker.

She leaned around him and kissed his mouth, rubbing one generous breast and then the other against his shoulder. "Mmmph," he said, trying to look over her shoulder at his papers, then as she stepped back he smacked his lips. "Jack Daniel's."

She made a monster face at him and said, "Ak, Balkan Sobranie. Lavenstein, the big destroyer of worlds." She sat down to his breakfast.

In the corral she saddled up Panama Red, a seven-year-old quarter horse, boxy and strong, with a deep Rodeo Association saddle. She needed a sensible mount. She put a packsaddle on Popcorn and rode off leading him, trying out her morning voice on a country-western song about wild times and fast women.

Her voice carried in the chill, still first air of the day. The light was dim behind the mountains that faced the ranch, and the sky was still royal blue in the west behind her. Cookie and Red and Popcorn dropped down into the valley of the Souk River, really a fast stream this high in the mountains. She didn't need to see the valley to know the grass was beginning again, the shooting stars were growing up through little patches of snow left in deep hollows, beavers were working the stream above the meadow, foxes were mating, owls were roosting up as they burped furry

3

bits, eagles and hawks were waiting for high light to show them mice and ground squirrels, and elk herds were moving out of the bottoms into the lay-ups above. Cookie knew the ranch like she knew her own body, and took the same joy in it. If something touched the ranch, she felt it in her, and on this morning she was cutting out a malignant growth.

Two hours west, down through Snoqualmie Pass on the interstate, the Pike Street market was lighted and bustling with greengrocers and butchers. Early-shift traffic was building toward the Boeing plant, and the occasional horn announced commuter peevishness. The dampened footfalls of the horses and their huffling cold-weather breathing were the only sounds here, as the three of them crossed the hard current and worked the switchbacks up the mountain face, finding more snow in the shadows of the spruces. She continued to sing as they climbed, and the horses—Red, at least—continued to listen.

They came out of the forest after the crest, breaking onto the long, wide reach of the Ellensburg Plateau, where the light was flat and strong. They turned along the edge of the trees and rode south a mile. Back into the trees to the west then, back toward the crest at a different angle, along the lip of a shallow arroyo that spilled out into the plateau. Cookie stopped singing.

She tied Red and Popcorn to saplings at the edge of a clearing and hoisted off Red's saddle. With the blanket like a serape over one shoulder and with the brush gun, she moved off through the trees. Before she left the clearing she pumped a cartridge up into the rifle's chamber.

It was early in the year and it was easy to walk without making a sound. Her father had taught her that. Her father had taught her almost everything she knew. Horses, weather, the ranch, men's eyes, hunting, fishing, then later he taught her drinking and cards and waiting, a real science. He'd peace-

4

officered and sheriffed enough, he said, and horses were too stupid to know they were being took advantage of, so he'd begun raising horses. But before that he'd covered this whole high country, in the prewar times when the lumbermills and the gold mines and the ranches had enough hard cases to work a sense of humor into anyone foolish or dull or curious enough to ride out and chastise them for their little lapses. Them along with some real, old-time badasses, and some professionals. For them you waited; the Long Science, he called it.

She lay along a root, the horse blanket under her, overlooking the arroyo and the carcass of a young horse, Chiliball. His neck and head lay at an unpleasant angle, from having been broken, and patches worn away from his flank showed how he'd been dragged. Several sets of claw marks showed what had dragged him.

The light came stronger and the air warmed slightly. Mice came out and foraged around her, birds banked through the trees. She waited.

Red screamed and kept on screaming. She was up and running, with no effort at quiet, rifle held low in one hand at the balance point, running to avoid roots and holes, ducking under branches. She saw Red first, dancing around, tethered to the sapling, trying to leap away from the awful bulk and smell of the monster. Popcorn was paralyzed with fright, white-eyed, shifting his feet and quivering. The bear was rocking on all fours and huffing, seeming to enjoy his bullying success. Cookie stopped.

"Fuck you!" she yelled. The bear spun. "Get the fuck out of there, you hairy sonofabitch!"

As Panama Red screamed, the bear hesitated, looked back to the skittering horse and away from the small, high-voiced creature. He rose to his combat height and he hesitated long enough.

She laid the ramp and notch under his ear, breathed once, and sent a round into his neck. The big Silvertip slug entered the hide and mushroomed under it, separating the skull from the spine, and the bear fell away from her. Red continued to scream.

Over's not over, not till it's over. Her father on waiting and on poking dead rattlers with short sticks. She put the rifle, new cartridge up but safety on, against a tree. The .41 held ahead of her, she walked toward the bear, keeping her field of fire clear of Red and Popcorn. Two bear's lengths away, she stood and waited again. She didn't need the revolver.

Red was goosy and his eyes white-rimmed all around, but he would be fine by the time they forded the Souk. Popcorn would be skittish for a week. Retying them, she came back with a knife and a whetstone, holding the revolver again. She prodded the bear with the knifepoint once and then put it away for the second time. Kneeling down, ruffling the coarse, rich fur of its jowls, she said, "You dumb bastard," with a note of sadness. But that was Cookie: She could cut steers and eat the mountain oysters, and still feel sorry for the unserviced cows. She rolled up her sleeves and started to skin the bear.

CHAPTER TWO

She loped into the corral, letting Red work himself out and coaxing Popcorn into sanity. Vern McKillip's four-by, with its bubble lights and SHERIFF emblem, was angled up to the barn, Vern asleep in the front seat until Red snorted.

"Easy, Red, it's the watchful eye of the law. Easy, boy."

Vern bolted upright, and out of the corner of her eye, she saw him replacing the hair he brushed forward over his hairline. He was Cute. He'd been Cute in fourth grade. "Popcorn, will you just get hold of yourself, dammit?" He was Cute now, twenty years past football and baseball, keeping up a little running and some iron, losing to the paunch. He was still smiling the sweet grin he had given her from the next seat in fourth grade, the same high-school halfback grin, heavier now around the same sweet face.

She tied off Popcorn and uncinched Red. Vern came along the fence toward her with the unhurried amble of a civil servant. She swung the saddle onto the top rail and started to comb out Red's winter coat. "How'd you ever get to be sheriff, Vern?" she called to him without looking. "You got some deep feeling for justice? It's odd, Vern, because I don't think you've got even one little speck of Wyatt Earp in you." She ducked under Red's neck and glanced back at Vern's fourth-grade grin. "You know that, Vern?" Time to cut back Red's coat for spring, she thought.

7

"Hell, Cookie, I'm a feared and respected lawman around some parts of town." He had a slow, soft voice. Cute.

"There's not but one part of Cle Elum, Vern. Wait now—are you talking about the schoolyard part?"

"They fear and respect me there, all right. John Law." He picked up her saddle easily and started into the barn.

"Seriously, Vern," she said without seriousness, "how did you persuade all five hundred active voters to make you sheriff? Why did you *want* to be sheriff?"

Vern stopped for a moment, thinking, and said over his shoulder, "Your old man, I guess. I wanted to be like him, I guess, so you'd dote on me as well."

"Hell, Vern, I do dote on you. You and old Red here." She slapped Red's haunch and moved around him.

"That's a fact, is it? I'll tell you what—that's a comfort. Now why didn't you tell me that twenty years ago?"

Her combing didn't falter. "Vern, you couldn't keep it in your pants long enough for me to get a little education, that's all. You knocked up that sweet little Darlene—best tits a sophomore cheerleader ever had, you always said—before I was through English 502. Take this bridle, you randy lawman. Popcorn, you sorry sonofabitch, go roll in some grass and feel sorry for yourself. Good luck."

They put away the saddle and tack, and when they came back out, a pot of coffee and two mugs sat steaming on the hood of Vern's four-by. Vern shook his head. "Nathan got star wars figured out yet?"

"He's a damned wonder, that Lavenstein. He is some smart."

"Cookie, what are you going to do about whatever killed that pony of yours?"

She kicked the poly-wrapped bundle at their feet. "Lie naked on him and have my picture took. You want a print, Vern?"

Vern shook his head and once more grinned the fourth-grade grin. Cookie punched him in the biceps, appreciatively, and walked inside with the coffeepot.

Vern followed.

"H'lo, Nathan. You need some help there?"

"Vern. Sure. You have any prime integers on you?"

"Sure do, Nathan. I'm giving the Celtics a five-point spread on the Lakers. Is that prime enough for you?"

"You're on. Twenty dollars."

"You can pay me Saturday night in Ellensburg."

"I'll buy you a drink out of the twenty you'll owe me."

"You two can bankroll each other without me. I smell like the inside of a bear." Nathan, who had seen the parcel packed on Popcorn, smiled without looking up. "I'm going to take a shower and go to town."

"Cookie," Vern asked, "will you last out the season with the hay you have?"

"I think so, Vern. I believe I've got enough in the canyon barn, but it's a good thought. I'll check it on my way into town. You want anything from town, Jewboy?"

Lavenstein looked up at her grinning face. "There's a list over on the counter. Try to get some salmon if it looks good."

"You want whiskey or a fancy woman? Do your paper a world of good, Nathan."

He turned to Vern. "Life on the ranch. Whoopie-ti-yi-yo."

"Git along, little dogie," Vern said, and heaved himself upright from a comfortable lean against the fireplace. "See you later, folks."

"You say 'Howdy' to Darlene for me, Vern," Cookie called.

As she braked her pickup outside the canyon barn, the poly bundle with the bearskin slid up against the cab. She got out and looked at it, blood and white fat against the thick film, smelling strongly of offal and meat through the wrapping. She

9

pulled it up in a corner of the bed, where it wouldn't flap when she hit the highway.

Inside the barn, she closed the door and latched it with the twist of fence wire nailed there, turned, and let her eyes adjust to the dim light and the high architecture of hay all around. Two stalls down, Vern leaned comfortably against another post.

Cookie unbuttoned her fresh canvas shirt, then the blue oxford shirt under it. She took them both off together. There was no chemise under them now. She stood, feeling the cool tingle her. It felt good, and she reached up with both hands and made slow circles with her fingers around her nipples, raising them, feeling even better. Vern watched her with a seriousness approaching the tragic, shifting against the post less comfortably now. "Gosh," he said.

Only Vern could look at a woman playing so satisfyingly with her breasts and say "Gosh." He really was Cute. She laughed out loud and rushed at him, knocking him into the hay.

CHAPTER THREE

She drove fast, using all five gears and working the shape of the road, and as she drove she gave herself a little smirk. You devil.

Coming up onto the plateau, she let the truck stretch out in fifth until the ground cover by the highway was a blur and only the mountains stayed firm. Across the grazing land to the east, a small herd of wapiti moved sedately, unconcerned. The day was clear and good ahead, all over the basin. The hay motes under her clothes pricked her skin, impishly, and the dampness in her was a private, pleasant feeling. Strong sunlight picked out the distant ranches and hay barns and the strings of cottonwood that made feathery spines wherever water cut into the flats.

Shit. Back through her rearview mirror, a blue-black pack of clouds darkened the western rim of the basin. April is a bad month for cheap contentment.

Cookie's arrival in town was always a series of stops and yells.

"Charlie! Charlie, come out here, you cheap bastard. When are you and Deneen going to come over and eat fancy Lavenstein cooking at my house? How's your boy? Tell him to stick the damn cast out the window, let the birds light on it, do something useful. No, really, he's okay? Willard will want to

11

know. I'll send some books over. *Lust Pigs of the Amazon* is a good one for the bedridden. Be good, Charlie."

Another slide of gravel, followed by the little pings of stones hitting hubcaps. "Harold, you sorry sonofabitch, you going to get that barn propped up anytime soon? Wind shifts and it'll come right down, I swear. You want me and the boys to come over middle of next week, get some fellas from Cle Elum, get that old thing fixed? Yeah, look at that damned cloud over there, Harold—that's not going to do you any damned good. You call."

Slide. Horn. "Millie! Pull up the window, Millie—I can't hear you worth a damn. Millie, can you finish that shirt by the twenty-ninth? Yeah, but the eggheaded sonofabitch is going back before his birthday. Oh, that's sweet of you, darlin'. You call me, hear? You need anything downtown? Okay, be good."

Rubber squeal of a U-turn. "Father Gogarty, how's the far-yonder business? Wilson and Willard and Bert and me need another hand for poker come Friday, and this time you can't put up souls for credit. You owe me a Rosary or a Hail Mary or some damned thing, and you owe a serious fifteen dollars to Willard. See you then. Be good. Just kidding, Father."

She walked into the Outrageous Taco, scratching at the folds of shirt that flared at her hips, muttering, "That'll teach me. Ought to put a bed down there, dammit."

"Wilson," she called across the restaurant, "you look terrible. You got a health problem, or are you just celibate? You hearing more noes than yeses, Weeelson?" In truth, Wilson looked just about as good or bad as he always did: small, thin, and myopic.

"Cookie, my girl, you look like you're getting it right along. You've got that special glow. How are you feeling in the mornings, old girl?" A Carolina drawl but sharp as whiskey.

"Just you hold on to that 'old girl' horseshit, Wilson. Keep it for Gigi. How's the book coming along?"

"Oh, we're working away. Got a lot of paper stacked up, but it's not a book yet. Haven't managed to make a clear connection between General Motors and the dissolution of the western world yet, but it's there somewhere. I don't work Charlie Bering hard enough, that's all."

"Charlie's going to kill you, come spring. You got him locked up like a monk out there."

Wilson cackled maniacally. "My God, Cookie, that's what he wants. That's what everybody wants—to bind themselves, body and soul, to a great idea. To be consumed by pious duty. Damn, Charlie should pay me for the karma I'm helping that boy lay down. Yessir." He grinned fiendishly.

"You're the strangest damned saint I ever talked to, Wilson."

"You talking to saints again, Cookie?"

"Only you, sweetmeat. I got troubles enough without saints. Which reminds me—we've got Gogarty for poker Friday night."

"That papist libertine. That parish diddler of youth . . ."

"So you lost ten dollars. Don't endanger your immortal soul, now."

"If I won big, I wonder if I could negotiate for the old sodomite's soul?" Again the fiendish grin.

"Hell, Wilson, you'd just love to be a villain, but you're too damned cute. Sanchez! How's a girl get fed around this beanery?"

They sat eating Sanchez's quesadillas and his fiery salsa, relieving them with Coronas. Wilson pulled a mouthful of beer and leaned over to start the Lionel train that Sanchez had made a track for, all around the wainscoting of the room. It hooted whenever it passed the kitchen. Sanchez loved it.

"What do you mean, come spring? It looks great out there now. A welcome relief from this mountain deep freeze."

13

"Sanchez, fry up some grits for this south-ren boy. Wilson, you haven't seen the last of winter. Just step outside and look back Seattle way. There's a pile of rain coming. Might be rain this time; it's just as likely to be a hooter of a blizzard next time. Don't breathe easy yet, Wilson. It's not over till it's over."

They stepped outside, toothpicks working on the carnitas, and walked to the end of the street, where they could look west. Not fast but steady, the dark clouds were eating up the western end of the plateau.

"Rain," she said, "this time."

Jim Stottlemeyer loved the bearskin. He was the taxidermist and doubled as one of the Grey Funeral Home morticians. The grisly single-mindedness of his life had struck some of the boys as unseemly, but it seemed about right to Cookie. They stood in the parking lot behind the home and rerolled the pelt.

"You ever stuff a person, Jim?"

The question didn't seem to disturb him. "No. Real hard to do that, Cookie. They don't—or wouldn't, I should say—skin out at all well. Bad pelt, weak hide, soft, too much fat. Especially some fat dude. Even just getting one of those fatties ready to inter . . . Don't get fat, Cookie. Makes everything hard, afterwards."

She rolled her eyes. "Shit, Jim, I'll start right now and get in trim for you. Jesus Christ."

"Just a suggestion."

"How's this going to look? I plan to spend some down-home fun time on this bearskin, Jim. You going to make this soft and shiny and manageable? It won't smell or anything, will it?"

"Oh, no. Nothing I do smells, Cookie."

She glanced back at the funeral home.

14

"Oh, stop it. It'll be good-looking. But if you want to roll around on a fur, go shoot yourself a sheep. Softer."

"How much am I going to owe you, Jim?"

"I'll tell you what. You bring me another elk, quartered and skinned out like you skinned that pelt for Millie, and we'll call it quits."

"Sounds light, Jim, but if that's good with you it's good with me." They shook hands.

"Here it comes." It had begun to sprinkle. "Let's get under cover. How long?"

"Two, three weeks, depending on . . ." He jerked his head over his shoulder at the funeral home.

"Right," she said. "Business. Be good, Jim."

The market had salmon. She could have gotten a major fish, enough to feed Willard and Bert in the bunkhouse too, but she was in the mood for Lavenstein's whole attention. Damned lasers. She bought a small salmon and asked for help at the liquor store picking out a bottle of champagne. Fuck lasers.

The rain was not hard but steady. Two days, maybe three. She thought to make sure the corral drained well.

She took the curves more cautiously, feeling for oil slick in the first hour of the rain. She waited for a car to pass going the other way and turned left into the ranch entrance.

Up the gravel road, after the first turn and before the bridge across the creek, a single figure with a blue backpack started up the rise, with almost two miles to go before the ranch house. Someone lost. Or a friend of Bert's or a backpacker. She slowed down to offer a ride.

She braked hard, leaped out, and ran to him. "Benjy!"

Soaked in the early spring rain, tired, shivering with cold, her brother had come home.

CHAPTER FOUR

He dropped the pack and his sister threw her arms around him, kissed him, tried to pick him up, to dance him around in the thin mud. He could not dance but clung to her, and they stood there in the rain.

"Aw, Benjy, you're shiv . . . hey, buddy, you're . . . hey, hey, it's all right, Cookie's here, Buddy, I'll take care of you. . . . Cookie's right here. . . ." She hugged him tighter, tighter still, felt his shoulders and chest buckle and heave with sobs, felt his hands desperate on her shoulders, holding on to her for life. Cookie had that, she could give him that, all right. She held him in the rain and patted his head and his shoulders the way she had when he was tiny, a baby. When he was nine and she was going off to college, leaving home for the classes her mother had arranged for her, he had cried like this and she had patted him with the same reassuring animal rhythm she used now, in the rain.

"Cookie's here, buddy." She turned him toward the truck, hoisted his pack on one shoulder, and got him inside. When their mother had left their father—or his ranch or his horsey country life or his private waiting silences—Cookie had known Benjy needed her, but she was too far away. She could not fail him now.

What disturbed her more than his pain was that she hadn't

17

felt it before she saw him. Without a belief in God or fate or anything but chance, Cookie still believed that she should have known he was in trouble, because they were part of one root. Why hadn't she known? How far had Benjy grown from her? She should have felt it. But that was Cookie, to deny herself the comfort of God and demand the responsibility of angels. As for her own troubles and hurts, they stayed inside with her guilt. She knew how she had hurt Benjy, how much she had stolen from him.

She had been her father's best son, his brightest pupil. By the time Benjy came, out of what mistake or plan she didn't know, there was no room for him in her father's heart.

No matter that Pete and Doris were not speaking to each other by the time Benjy was three, or that Doris shaped Benjy to be wholly unlike Pete, using him—if not maliciously, then carelessly—against his own father. Or that she took him away when she left. Took him to Washington Heights, overlooking the lake, and Benjy was given all the bribes she and her new man could offer a boy with furtive eyes.

Cookie wrapped him in a blanket from behind the seat and started over the bridge, up the grade, and around the shoulder of the ridge for home. No, she didn't count all that or Benjy's troubles with the law, the sprees and joyrides and pot busts. Pete came not to speak of Benjy, kept an embarrassed silence. She knew what had caused it: She had stolen Pete's love from Benjy, she had been the best son. Her troubles were his.

She helped him out of the truck and onto the porch. She hugged him again under the low roof, rain drumming above them, and opened the door before him. Benjy was home.

Lavenstein rose immediately, and with one worried frown applied his famous concentration to nurturing: a chair slid before the fire, a fresh blanket, a kettle on the range. He left, reappeared with a towel, dry shirt, pants, socks, sweater, and while Cookie helped Benjy out of his sodden clothes, Lavenstein brought a bottle of Jack Daniel's and two glasses. Things in order, he poured the bourbon and put the glasses into Benjy's and Cookie's hands, then brought a towel and robe for her. Concentration. He turned to the range and began to make coffee.

Cookie left the room in unusual modesty and returned in a moment, wearing the robe. She began to rub her brother's hair with the towel, gently, as if she could press some of her strength into him. In the firelight, as she straightened Benjy's hair with her fingers, Lavenstein watched worried thoughts scroll and change on her face. He could see every line of her forty-two years, laughs and worries, mostly for other people, mostly for Benjy. She was a beautiful woman.

But he wondered now why they did not speak, what held Cookie back. Nothing else did. He brought the coffee, set it down. Taking the empty glass from Benjy's hand, he put a mug into it. "Ben," he said, "what's the problem?"

Benjy looked down, around the room, into the fire.

"Ben, I know there's a problem. You're here, you're banged up. What's going on?"

Cookie nodded, hopelessly. While Benjy had changed, they had both seen the scabbed shoulder and the yellow-blue bruise that ran down his ribs. Her mouth moved without words; her hand continued to smooth his hair. She was like this with no one else, but this inertia would wear away into action, and Lavenstein hoped no one had done this to Ben.

"Ben," he said.

"I went in," he began suddenly, "crashed. Plane burned. All the stuff went up with it, fuel tanks went up, bang—"

"Where?" Cookie asked.

"—like it was the Fourth of July, like some damned movie. Whoom. You should have seen it go."

19

"Where?"

"Near the Mexican border, down around Laredo. I was hedgehopping, zooming up those canyons. . . ." Ben had flown since he was fifteen, starting in his stepfather's Cessna. He had been grounded several times and had crashed before. Cookie had been with him at the hospital for weeks, and his traction frame was still in the barn somewhere. He had even flown supply planes for army intelligence in Southeast Asia. It was his one skill.

"What happened?" Lavenstein asked.

He looked at the fire, the floor.

"Tell him," Cookie said.

"I was flying a Long-EZ. They're not supposed to pick those things up on radar, but they did. Picked me right up, chased me all over hell, and they were good. I shook them, though. I'm almost sure I shook them."

"What happened?"

"I just augered in, is all. I came up out of that one canyon and over the rim, and there was this big fucking tree—what the hell was it doing there?" His voice was a little boy's, breaking on the injustice of the tree. "No damned business being in the middle of the fucking desert, for Christ's sake, and I put a wing right through it and went down, lucky to get out. Whoom—those fuel tanks. Should have turned the ignition off right away. First damn rule, you know?

"Give me another drink, will you? This has been a bitch. Bad day, bad couple of days, Cookie."

Lavenstein wanted to keep Ben's focus away from Cookie until they found out what they were dealing with. There was more to the story. Once Cookie started to baby him, his story would change; he would want nothing but care.

Lavenstein spoke. "Ben, why are you here? Why aren't you in a hospital? Why didn't you just call us from down there? When did this happen?"

"Monday, last Monday. How about another jolt of that? Happened on Monday and I got to a town on Tuesday and made some calls, and I've been getting here ever since."

"Eight days. What calls?"

"Cookie, I'm real tired and I've got to talk to you. Hey, Nathan, can I talk to my sister? Do you mind? It's just family stuff. We've got to talk."

Cookie looked at Lavenstein, asking, but he shook his head, just a slight motion. He could see she was coming out of her mothering panic. "Tell it, Benjy. Tell us what's coming off here."

"I just want to talk to you, Cooks. I can—"

"This is bad, Benjy. You need more than me. Spit it out, Bebo."

He took another swallow of the Jack Daniel's and fumbled with the glass. Lavenstein started to speak, but Cookie put her hand on his shoulder and he closed his mouth.

"Get it over with, Benjy," she said. "I'm right here."

"These guys, this investment group, made some deals and set up some deliveries. I was just running some packages for them, you know? I was just delivering—easy in, easy out."

"Oh, Jesus, Benjy."

"It was all set up, nice as you please. These guys had it all ready; I loaded up and got out. One day, done, out."

"Jesus, Benjy. Flying drugs across the border for the goddamned mob? Are you really that crazy?"

"It wasn't the mob. Wasn't mob at all. A group of investors, upscale guys, bunch of goddamned dentists from Charleston, West Virginia, set it up. They had charts and everything, rates of return against time and investment, comparison to stock market return, risk factor. Computer stuff. In color."

Lavenstein shook his head in disbelief. Cookie turned away.

CHAPTER FIVE

"These investors, Ben, they're in the East, and they know about this?"

"Oh, yeah, yeah, they know about it, all right. They sure as hell know about it. Give me some more of that, Nate."

Lavenstein ignored him, put the bottle on the floor. "You told them, when you called. What's their position now?"

"Position? Position? They've got a position, they do. They are pissed. Not like you'd get pissed or I'd get pissed, but pissed. I have discounted their profit posture. Get that? I fly into a fucking tree, damn near burn up my ass, and they are pissed that I have discounted their posture, whatever that means.

"I told them, I said, Look, you guys, I'm really sorry and all that, I almost got fucking killed for you, but that's the way it goes in the friendly skies, and you might look into who tipped the federales or the feds about the route I flew for you bastards. If I hadn't had a big cockpit bubble and if I hadn't been twisting my neck off looking for something like this, I wouldn't have seen the sonofabitch back there, shadowing me, waiting for me to land. Who was that, huh? And I lost him. I'm sure I lost him. Fed. Federale. Whoever."

He reached down and pulled back the bottle by the neck. He poured the glass full and offered it to Cookie. "You want some, Cooks?" She shook her head, so he tipped back a third of the glass and filled it full again, keeping the bottle in his hand.

"Whoever. Lost him." He looked into the fire, beginning to stare.

Lavenstein wanted to get it out of him, all of it. "So you told them. What happened?"

"So I told them: they, she, this bitch named Trotter who's head of the group—get this, the Floss Group, Charleston, West by God Virginia. Oh, Jesus, that's sweet." He was shaking now. Cookie felt his shaking and his fear. He was afraid to tell them something; whatever it was frightened him even more.

"Benjy. What happened? No, Benjy." She took the glass from him, then the bottle, still mother but firm. "Tell it."

"They'd call me back, she said. Stay there and they'd call me back. I had a motel room down there, awful little place, bad TV. Stay put, they said. We'll call."

"Did they?"

"Sure. Late that night. They wanted to recoup their loss, and I was the source of loss so I would recoup it, I guess."

"How?"

"Three flights, new plane, new route, less pay."

"And."

"And what? I told them to fuck off. Fuck off, bitch, I've had it with you toothies. I laid my life on the line; I'm out.

"But that wasn't good enough, she said. I had responsibilities, she said, that I must discharge. They couldn't allow my incompetence to jeopardize their investment. Can you believe that crap? I told them, Look, I said, take off, bitch. Do more dentures to make it up; you aren't making it up with my ass.

"I'm real tired, Cooks. This bores me. Let's call it a day, hey?"

24

He wasn't bored. He was tired, and the bourbon was hitting him, but he was wired and scared. He was close to something.

"They said what?"

"They said shit."

"Ben," Lavenstein said, with as much heat as he ever used, "maybe Cookie is more patient with this than I am. But you need some help, right now. You're not getting it this way."

"Come on, Benjy," she said more softly. "What then?"

"They said they couldn't allow me to back out of my contract at this time. The bitch said that I would complete the new contract to bring everything in line with their original investment.

"I said no. No way. She said yes. I said, Look, bitch, you don't want the guys who were trailing me to know who you are, right? I mean, I know every one of you guys and where you live, see? You try to tell me just what to do and I tell the FBI or the narcs what your little toothy group is up to for high returns and good posture."

"So?"

"So she wasn't so pleased then, not this much. She shut up a second. That stopped her. I put in a little zinger then. Little zinger. I said, You know, not all of that stuff burned and it's out there and only I know where it is. That stopped her, all right. So you can just lay off Ben C. Culler, is all."

This time she let him have the bourbon. She knew the rest, though she wished she didn't. "Is there anything left in the plane?"

"Hell, no. Should have seen that thing go up. Whoom." His hand fluttered up unsteadily with the explosion.

"And she said . . . ?"

"She said, Okay, would discuss the matter with colleagues. I should stay put. Again.

"What for? I asked her. Just get another boy to deliver your

25

packages. No, she said, she was sure they could make a deal that was Mutually Ad-van-ta-gee-ous. Sure. Well, maybe they could, I thought. Watched reruns most of the day. Then I started to get a little, you know, paranoid. Wary."

"Scared." Lavenstein filled it in.

"Yeah, scared. I guess. I got my pack and went out the back window of the motel. Didn't check out. Sneaked out over a rise and crossed the road a mile or so down and came around the other side and watched. With those little binoculars. You know? Jesus, they're so nice. Cooks, I ever tell you how much I like those little things? That was real sweet of you. Cookie gave me these. . . ." He reached for his pack and spilled the bourbon glass, the sweet amber smell heavy around them. "Aw, shit. Look that." He was just about to crash.

"Go on, go on," she said, tightening her hand on his shoulder.

"Lay up there in the weeds, no' many weeds, an' watched. Car come, stop at motel office, back to car get something, walk real careful down my room, kick in door, bang like that. Bang, door. Mut'l Ad-van-ta-geous, shit. Go in. Come out. Leave in car, not pay for door." His head was oscillating slowly, like a metronome in oil.

Cookie turned his head and steadied it in both hands before her. "Ben, listen to me, Ben. Do they know you're here? Do they know about this place, about us, about where you'd go?"

Benjy's face broke into a drunken caricature of sorrow and hopelessness, like a five-year-old who wakes to a wet bed. "Cookie," he sobbed between her hands, his lips fished out with the intensity of her holding. "Think so. Think I told before. Gon' come hurt me, Cookie. Don't l'em hurt Benjy, Cookie."

Of course not. She drew his face into her chest and held him, pat pat, pat pat, pat pat. Lavenstein got up and pulled the curtains, locked the door, sat down beside her with his own hand on her shoulder, and they all sat there with the smell of bourbon and applewood fire, Benjy's sobs, and the fire's small noises, which went on for some time before it burned down and Benjy was asleep.

CHAPTER SIX

Some horses shy at the ford. The curling rush of water confuses their depthless vision. But Searle never shied, not at crossing the river or at anything but rattlesnakes. As long as Cookie kept him off the Minetailing Trail, where there were always rattlers, he was the steadiest, most imperturbable mount she had, almost somber. But now he shied. Benjy sawed at the reins, cursed, flapped his stirrups into Searle's ribs.

Cookie turned Red back from midstream, dropping Popcorn's lead over his packsaddle so he would continue to the far bank. "Easy, Searle." She leaned over and rubbed the big brown hunter behind the ears, where he liked it. "Easy, you big preppie."

"Don't oversteer him, there, Benjy. Just let him go. He knows the trail better than you do. He feels your nerves and it spooks him." She was talking to Benjy but addressing the horse, looking into its big muddy eye and drawing her words out in a rhythm, low. "Get back into cowboying slow, Bebo, take it easy, take this trip for the ride, okay? I'm here."

They took the same trail up the mountain face she had used on the morning she killed the bear, the switchback trail you can see from the ranch house porch, in bare places, until it is lost in the pines and spruces of the forest that runs along the crest. From the ranch house, on a spur of ridge that separates two pastures, north and south, the mountain seems to rise straight up from the Souk, whose rush south is dented by the intrusion of the ridge. The rock of the ridge makes the ford; the seasons of the Souk, flooding and receding, make the pastures rich. Morning comes a little late in the valley, but with your feet propped up on the porch railing and a drink in your hand, the evening sun lights up the flat plane of the mountain across the way in a grand manner. Pete had loved the place, left it seldom, and Cookie had helped him back from the hospital so he could die here.

Halfway up the mountain, they took a small trail that angled south from one of the north-trending switchbacks. It looked like an early, rougher try at the switchback they were riding but switched north itself in about sixty yards. They rode the contour, keeping about the same elevation, for half a mile, then dipped east into a pocket with its own meadow, a clear lake several hundred yards long flanked by marsh on both sides, and a cabin at the end. It was for this secret place, and not for the bigger cut of the Souk, that Pete Culler's—now Cookie Culler's—spread had been called Hidden Valley Ranch. Smoke rose from the cabin chimney, and they rode along the shoreside trail, becoming part of the postcard fantasy.

They hitched the horses to the porch posts. A voice from inside, speaking peevishly but calmly, as if admonishing a dog that was sleeping on a chair he always slept on but shouldn't, an old man's voice, said, "I had no intention of seeing you for another month. This winter is not done yet, and I had set my mind on peace and reflection until spring does appear. I suppose, though, that I am not so bitter about seeing you that I will not share a cup of coffee. If you have brought coffee. I appear to have used up mine." The door opened and, indeed, a dog did come out, and it looked like the sleepy, indifferent kind of dog that slept on chairs. It stepped out ignoring the visitors, a pose better in many ways than Lavenstein's.

"Wilfred," Cookie called through the logs in her normally loud voice. "I just came up here to see if you were dead. We smelled something dead about a week back and said, Damn if that's not old Wilfred Bottoms, who has died of masturbation. He's up there moldering away, and we better plant the old sonofabitch. I got a shovel somewhere here, Wilfred—the Wilfred Bottoms Memorial shovel, we were going to call it. After."

The door opened wider and, slightly more peevishly, the voice came out: "When I plan to die, of masturbation or boredom, I will hike down to your place and let you know."

A tall, gaunt man stepped out, dressed in boots, Levi's, red suspenders over the faded red of a union suit, and a stained Resistol silver-belly hat. An Indian blanket was draped over his shoulders, and he carried a book. His walrus mustache, a pattern seen in tintype photos, moved and twitched when he talked. It was also the mustache seen, on a younger man, beside Pete Culler in a yellowing photo of a ranger muster on Cookie's wall. "You are a disrespectful child. Hello, Benjy. That is Benjy, isn't it?" Wilfred seemed to take little interest in anything but Cookie and the pack she was unlashing from Popcorn's Mexican tree. "You should be more respectful by half. I'm probably even your real father, you know. I don't even remember half the mares I serviced in my days at stud. Here, let me help you with that."

"I got it."

"Independent child too. Hell, I beat Pete's time with all his women, probably with your mama too. No offense, Benjy," he said over his shoulder, not looking at Benjy but working on the lashing, getting in the way.

"Get the hell out of there, Wilfred. You'll strangle yourself with the damned line."

31

"A vile child. I'm sorry I brought you into this world. What'd you bring me?"

"Laxative. Big size."

"Ha. You should be as regular and fine-running as my system is. Cookie, you can expect my next dump at sunrise tomorrow as surely as you can expect the sun."

"Do I have to wait around and see?"

"My system has refined, gotten better over the years. What'd you bring me?"

"Stop fiddling with that damn line, Wilfred. Here, take this one in and I'll bring on the other."

The interior of the cabin was filled with books of all sizes, all types, on floor-to-pitch-line shelves of roughsawn. There were stacks of magazines new and old; a bed neatly made with a red Hudson's Bay blanket; a large two-vise workbench, which also, it seemed, served as kitchen counter (a kitchen knife, a pot, and a basket of potatoes sat on it) and laboratory (a half-dissected frog was pinned open to a split log face beside a bookmarked edition of *Biology* by Moon, Mann, and Otto). The center of the room was ruled by a Regal Atlantic kitchen stove, huge and ornate. Before its warmth, which touched Cookie's face and the backs of her hands, sat an age-polished morris chair, flanked by several stacks of books, their pages marked with leaves and the tails of mice, and a table with a kerosene lamp. A water kettle was just coming to the boil on the stove.

"You are slow, a backward sort. Open this up, will you? Where's the damned coffee?" Wilfred cleared the workbench, carrying the frog—which seemed to be fresh—carefully to the table beside the chair. The tarps folded back, he sorted through the provisions, clucking and humming to himself happily. The coffee was found. He handed it to Cookie without a glance, and she began to make coffee in a drip pot on the stove, while Wilfred went through cans, packages. "New

York boy still down there?" He held up a tin of chopped chicken liver.

"Put it in special for you," Cookie replied.

"Hebrews eat strange but well," he commented to no one in particular.

Dried beans of several sorts, flitches of bacon, books, several copies of *Penthouse,* a large plastic bottle of a ketchup much admired by Wilfred ("Look at that—no waiting"), hard candy, three boxes of .30/06 ball cartridges.

"Am I expecting the invasion of the Hun?" He held them up.

The coffee was making; Cookie turned to Wilfred. "We've got to talk serious," she said.

"Outside," Wilfred said, and they walked out the door, leaving Benjy, who had not been noticed since the remark about his mother, to gather himself and follow them. They walked to one end of the porch and, in a ritual dance known to paleolithic hominids and horse traders, looked up at the sky together, looked out at the lake with slow, parallel gazes, and when Wilfred said, "Well?" they both squatted down close to the fir planks and watched the grain, as if it would tell them something. Wilfred fished out a pocketknife and began to clean his nails. They spoke low and casually, as if what they said had only minor consequence, which they both knew was not true or they would not be dancing the ritual, but that is the way they spoke.

"We got trouble. Complicated stuff," Cookie began. "Some fellas are after Benjy. Mean to hurt him, maybe kill him."

"He deserve it?"

"Probably. By their lights, yeah, he does. He got mixed up in some runs across the border with some get-rich eastern folks. Piled up their plane, lost their goods, got scared, threatened to expose them. They don't like it."

"Sense. Sense," Wilfred said disgustedly, commenting on the lack of it.

"He also told them some of the stuff wasn't burned in the crack-up." Wilfred made an interrogative noise. "No. It's all burned; he was just trying for leverage. They want to know where it is. Wouldn't believe it isn't there, now, if he told them. They want the location, maybe they want him to run more stuff, and they probably want him dead."

"They send anybody?"

"Arizona. Sent some boys to his motel. Benjy had bolted and watched them from the weeds."

Wilfred humphed through his mustache.

"He's pretty sure they know about the ranch."

"What kind of talent they going to send out?"

"I think they're amateurs. They're a bunch of dentists from West Virginia, in the high-risk, high-gain speculation business. They'll maybe send out some cheap muscle."

"Eastern. City guns."

"Have to be."

"How long?"

"Probably asking around town now. I don't know. Maybe they'll let it go. Maybe not. We need some time to figure it. Need to keep Benjy . . ."

"From getting his pecker blowed off. Boy got the sense of a grasshopper. This isn't Eye-talian stuff, is it?"

"Ask Benjy. I don't think it is."

"They'd have done a better job in the first place. Probably not."

"This okay with you? Can you handle anything that comes up? There's an extra piece in the pack for Benjy, if you want." Benjy could hear them, but it didn't matter. Wilfred was in charge up here.

"Good Lord, no. Be twirling it around his finger and shoot me. Them things are dangerous. Can he use it?"

34

"He was in the army."

Another filtered humph. "He learned to fly helicopters and airplanes and shoot standing up to targets. I mean can he use it?"

"He's a good man, Wilfred. He's Pete's son."

Wilfred had the good sense not to say who Pete's son really was. He cut the matter off by turning and speaking directly to Benjy for the first time. "Can you read?"

Benjy, confused, nodded.

"You're gonna need it up here."

CHAPTER SEVEN

Julia Child called it dogwork, the slicing-and-dicing vegetable preparation. Lavenstein enjoyed it. It was pure dexterity, wholly unmathematical, reassuringly practical, a meditation in skill applied. The big J. A. Henckels cook's blade started slowly and picked up rhythm as the burnished orange of a carrot fed into it, transformed from cylinder to rolling disks with a woodpecker staccato. One carrot, two, three, and he gathered the mounting pile with the thick back of the blade and finished the carrots.

The ends of four Spanish onions, root and stem, went into his stock pile. He passed the knife lightly around one longitude of each and, with a flick of the blade's square chin, loosened and unwrapped the outer layer with the skin. This, too, went into the stock pile. He clove a shallow section from each end, making a flat that sat firm on the chopping surface and bore the same transformation into concentrically compassed disks, thin enough to become translucent the moment heat and butter touched them.

Soup, the comfort of the kitchen. Lavenstein gathered celery, parsley, turnips, cans of extravagantly labeled Italian tomatoes, dried leaves of bay, wisps of thyme from window pots, indulging himself in handwork, escaping the black-on-white numbers on his desk.

He pulled down one of the bound sprigs of serrano pepper pods from the ceiling hooks as he watched the black Trans Am come up the gravel road and pull across the hitching rail before the porch as if it were a curb. The car had rental plates and an Avis sticker. The driver sat looking around him for a full minute before he turned the engine off. By that time Lavenstein had diced the peppers and lifted them into his small skillet with butter and a few of the onion slices. Now he used a curving butcher knife to peel off thin, angled cuts from the two chuck steaks that would make his soup base. The driver got out and walked around his car, kicking the tires but looking up under his thick brows at the barns and the outbuildings. He stepped onto the porch and knocked.

Lavenstein had washed his hands carefully, and he came to the door, drying them. "Good morning," he said. "Are you lost?"

Twenty-two trying to look twenty-eight, the driver had gel-styled brush-cut hair, sandy blond, maybe bleached, pale nightlife skin, eyes that touched everything appraisingly, even rudely but did not meet Lavenstein's eyes. "Ey," he replied, revealingly. He wore a short-waisted gabardine jacket with pleats and shoulder pads, pleated pants narrowed at the cuffs, light-gray shoes with delicate toes. He rocked up and back on his toes as if he were cold, and he kept his hands in the big patch pockets of the jacket.

"May I help you?" Lavenstein watched him with interest.

"Yeah. Yeah." Eyes darting past Lavenstein into the house.

Lavenstein turned his head as if to follow the eyes. "Would you care to come in?"

"Sure. Yeah, thanks," and the Boy almost walked past him.

Inside, Lavenstein pulled out a chair for him at the table near the stove. "Have a seat," he said.

The Boy nodded and sat down without speaking.

"What brings you up this way? Looking to board some horses, buy some stock?"

Still looking, nervous, he replied, "Yeah. I might."

"Folks that run the ranch will be back soon."

"You don't, like, work on the horses or cows or anything like that?" Lavenstein could almost place the nasal eastern accent.

"I just stay here"—Lavenstein pointed to the pile of papers by the fireplace—"to work."

"Paperwork. Yeah. Accountant or something." It wasn't a question, more an appraisal for later: "He was an accountant or something."

"Look. Like, you know these people run the farm here?"

"Pretty well."

"Sure. You know, like, Benjy Culler, he come around lately? We're friends from some stuff we were doing and I was out here, like, close, and dropped by to say Ey."

"Benjy's around. I don't know where right now."

"He be back with the farm boss?"

"I don't know."

"Yeah. Well. Maybe he'll be back, ey?"

"Maybe. I'm just cooking."

"Sure."

Nathan turned and picked up the butcher knife to take another slice off the chuck. The Boy jerked in his chair, making a noise, and said, "Ey! Put that thing down."

Lavenstein looked over his shoulder. The Boy had a revolver in his hand, snub-nosed, no sight, small caliber, taped handle. Lavenstein didn't know much about guns, but it didn't strike him as a very well made piece of equipment. Of course, he was used to J. A. Henckels Twinbrand grade.

"Philadelphia," Lavenstein said. "You're from Philadelphia, that's it."

The Boy looked puzzled, pointing the muzzle of the gun up and down Lavenstein's long frame.

"I did graduate work in Philadelphia. Lived on Kenshaw Street. I knew. I could hear it in your voice."

"Brockton. I live over on Brockton Avenue. Ey. Don't mind this." He waved the gun but didn't take it off Lavenstein completely. "Like, knives, they make me real nervous, you know? Don't like 'em. Nasty little fuckers. Big knife like that, you know? Just leave that fucker down."

Lavenstein continued to cut another slice, feeling the little revolver wavering over him. "Oddest thing," he said. "I was just making a Philly steak. Can you believe that? I've got the steak, the cheese right over here, if you can stand me cutting it, and here's the steak, good stuff. I've got some seeded rolls right here—see? Hey, you wouldn't want one, would you?"

Shrug, gun still out, pointed down but not entirely away. "Ey. I could do it. Sure."

Lavenstein did it right. Toasted the rolls while he sliced the cheddar thin. The little Saturday night special came up again while he cut. He pushed the onions and peppers toward the rim of the skillet and turned up the flame. When it was hot enough he laid in the steak slices and let them sizzle only so long, flipped them, sizzle, mixed them with the peppers and onions, sizzle, almost ready.

In a small flurry, he scooped the hot steak into the rolls and laid on the cheese. It began to melt almost immediately. Satisfactory. "Kind of small," he said. "I'll put on some more." The Boy nodded.

He handed him the sandwich in a napkin. "You want a plate?"

"Nah," the Boy said shortly, and eyed the sandwich.

Lavenstein shook the skillet horizontally with one hand, making a noise on the grating. "Keeps the steak from sticking. You ever make an omelet? Same thing."

"Nah."

"Hey," he said, "be careful with this sub; you may not be used to peppers. Pretty strong." He held up the sandwich in a Philadelphia toast and took a big bite, smiling around it.

40

"Peppers. Huh. You kidding? You ever eat, like, real Italian peppers? Ey." The Boy took a huge bite.

After three or four chews with no swallow, his eyes opened wide and tears sprang from them; his mouth came open and with it came a sound, of pain and surprise, from around the masticated wad. He started to rise, reaching for his mouth.

Wait for the ball, watch it come, and stroke to the follow-through, body, shoulder, and body; a backhand shot. Lavenstein stroked from his wide shoulders with the form that had made him captain of the Shaker Heights High School tennis team, '62, '63: keeping the racket face closed and bringing it up for what would have been a wicked overhand spin. The hot skillet caught the Boy full in the face, grease side, making a dull gonging sound as it rebounded slightly from his pale forehead.

The revolver clattered onto the floor before the Boy hit it, blood already spurting from his nose and brow. Lavenstein picked it up and put it in the towel drawer, watching with distaste the spreading red pool as it mixed with the grease. He sighed and got out a spray bottle of kitchen cleaner. He supposed he should take the bolus of steak and bread and peppers out of the Boy's mouth. He might choke and die. Lavenstein ate his Szechuan Philly steak sub with one hand while he cleaned up with the other, pushing several paper towels under the Boy's unmoving head to catch further blood.

When he had finished cleaning, he went to the pantry and brought back a roll of gaffer's tape and some newspaper. He very well might choke and die, thought Lavenstein. He finished the sandwich before he turned the Boy over and shook his head until the bite came out. His jaw felt as if it might be broken. Maybe not. He took everything out of the Boy's pockets and patted him down, finding a switchblade in his sock. Philadelphia. He used the newspaper and the gaffer's tape to truss him up securely without stopping circulation,

41

exhibiting the single-minded concentration for which Lavenstein was noted. The Boy was beginning to groan. He gagged him with a dish towel, reflecting that if his jaw was broken it wouldn't do it any good, and dragged him onto the side porch, where the garbage was kept. It was a cool day but not bitterly cold.

Lavenstein returned to his soup.

CHAPTER EIGHT

Smelling of horse and pine and new air, Cookie clattered through the door, with a great banging of boots against the sill and scraping of horseshit, and a series of familiar epithets at high volume. It was her way of sweeping down the staircase.

"Goddamned stuff is everywhere. Shit machines. Cookie Culler's Fertilizer Factory. Do you know, Lavenstein, how rich this little place is? All those dumb damn horses eating, eating, shitting, shitting, producing what causes brussels sprouts and wheat and raisins to leap up out of the ground. Makes you dizzy. We got here enough prime agricultural enhancer to cover the whole A-rab peninsula. If we spread it out. Lavenstein! Culler becomes a world power, selling shit to the A-rabs. Serves them and me right. I sell them shit at exorbitant prices, big international leverage deals. Culler the K. I take hostages. Four or five mullahs, make them muck out the barn, except for the Ayatollah; he gets the chicken house."

She was shouting from the bathroom now, sitting on the toilet with the door open.

"The carrot and the stick. You threaten them with some kind of destruction. The Lavenstein Pigfat Laser, destroys cities, denies paradise. We bargain for a new irrigation system and a bigger hot tub, buy fancy boots with silver toes, move to New York, hell, I don't know." She was about shouted out. "Who belongs to that black bomb out front? What's for lunch?"

Lavenstein finished arranging papers in neater piles and lifted up the lid of a pot to smell. "Soup and corn bread. New soup; better tomorrow but good today."

She came back into the room, hitching up her Levi's with difficulty, the .41 weighing the left side down. She unsnapped the holster and put it on the counter as she came up behind Lavenstein and put her arms around him. He could feel her body against him, from knees to forehead; she was nestling a little closer, a little needier than simple lust warranted. She was worried. He turned and kissed her. She lifted herself to him, mouth to mouth, but he knew it was holding she wanted. He was not a theoretical physicist for nothing. He held her and they rocked gently, leaning against the counter, and she was quiet for a while.

"What's that noise?" she finally asked.

"Here." Lavenstein disengaged himself and opened the towel drawer. "You might put this in your back pocket." He gave her the revolver, cheap bluing and gray tape.

"Where'd you get this nasty little thing? Damn little twenty-two toy pistol."

"No toy. That's the weapon of choice for liquor stores and knocking off rival businessmen. No-print tape on the handle and trigger, no front sight or hammer spur, filed off not to catch coming out of your pocket, disposable like Kleenex. Bang, bang, drop it, walk away."

"Where'd you learn about stuff like this, Jewboy?"

"You've been in the country too long, Dale. I'm city."

She looked toward the side porch and gestured sideways with her head. "There?"

"The first visitor. A young man from the city of brotherly love."

44

Cookie questioned him with a look.

"Philadelphia," he replied. "An inexpensive beginning. What you'd expect from an investment group?"

She was already on her way to the door, opening it cautiously, finding the boy. He was trussed up in the newspaper and the silver-gray tape. The blood caked over the dish towel gag was softened and puddled by his tears. He shivered and blinked constantly, whimpering, squinching his streaming eyes.

"Jesus," Cookie said. She was dumbfounded. "What's wrong with him? I mean beside his nose and cheekbone. Whoof. You get kicked by a horse?" she asked him, as if he could answer.

"He got something in his eyes."

Cookie leaned over and sniffed at him. He had wet himself and had shit his pants too, but that was nothing at the Culler Fertilizer Factory. There was also . . . "Chilies. How'd this little fella get chilies and grease all over his face, Lavenstein?" She was almost accusing him.

"He got in the way of a skillet."

"Hell." She looked at the boy's face and winced. "Maybe I'd better carry a skillet instead of that forty-one. This boy needs a doctor. Why didn't you call Babs and Chuck?" Who ran the ambulance.

"Not unless you want to explain everything about Benjy. It's your decision, not mine, Cookie. How do we work this?"

Cookie bit her lip, contemplatively, sadly, uncertainly. She ran warm water in a bowl and hunkered down beside the boy, bathing his eyes with a sponge, wiping away what she could without touching his ruined nose or flattened cheekbone. She was thorough, gentle, unknotting the towel slowly and laying it aside, sponging away the blood that had clotted under it. She, too, thought the jaw might be broken. She tended to the boy who had come for her brother as she would any animal on the place, with her gentlest instinct. But that was Cookie.

45

Lavenstein knew what she would do. He put some corn bread and some fruit in a plastic bag. She threw a blanket around the boy and closed the door on him with one more look. Lavenstein handed her the bag, and she took it without thinking.

"I've got to look at some fence on the front range. Call Vern. Ask him to watch for me along the highway and beep for me. We can work something out, get this boy to a hospital, get him out of here." She was not looking at Lavenstein. Her eyes moved around the room abstractedly, settling on a photo of Pete at a branding, standing in his stovepipe chaps and wiping his hatband with a bandanna. She walked over to it, looked at it a moment, said, "Call Vern, Nathan, and . . . I told you that, didn't I?"

Lavenstein moved toward her, but this jarred her reverie. She walked around the counter, avoiding him, and out the door. "Be back," she said, without looking.

In a few minutes she rode by the window, a knot of concern over her eyes. She had saddled Rambler, a white gelding, and Lavenstein could see her clearly until she loped around the upgrade curve toward the ridgeback. She had taken a coil of fence wire, and her heavy gloves were in her belt along with her fence pliers. But he could see that she had forgotten the corn bread on a post beside the corral. Her Smith & Wesson lay on the counter beside him. He picked it up and thought of driving after her. But Vern would be there. And she needed time alone in the open.

CHAPTER NINE

The Souk River cuts south at Cle Elum, then turns west to tumble over Snoqualmie Pass, in blended company with a dozen other small rivers that splash and seep and sluice down toward the Sound. The pair of north and south ridges holding the Souk and the center slice of Hidden Valley Ranch extend not a thousand meters, are perhaps three hundred meters deep. The highway from Snoqualmie to Cle Elum and northeast to Ellensburg closes with the Souk and crosses it on a steel bridge seven miles above the ranch. The highway, Route 109, is a line of concrete painted over the backs and across the cusps of round hills that jostle close enough to make a rolling, rising plain cresting at the lip of the great Ellensburg bowl. In this massive, flat biosphere, more dish than bowl, grows alfalfa of famous lushness, and hardy fruit that sucks its sweetness from the teeth of long winter. In the fall, 109 is loud with the labored whine of hay trucks hauling away the greenish-gold blocks shaved from the face of Ellensburg's plain. It was quiet in the early spring, as Cookie rode the roundbacked hills near it.

She looked for Vern's four-by, black and white and gold, with its oversized gumball light, searchlights, and whip antenna. Not yet. The sky was mottled gray. The horse-blanket lining in her denim jacket felt good in the wind, and she had

47

put on roping gloves when she came out of the trees.

She had ridden up across the ridge and then north, checking the lines of fence for winter damage, trying not to think. The ground was soft after yesterday's rain, and Rambler picked his footing. She had found a few breaks and spliced them with new wire. She had found a few rotted posts, and a sagging section that spanned a range freshet. Each required some rude engineering with whatever material was at hand on a bare hillback: rocks, windfall limbs, old parts of the fence, wire from the roll lashed to her saddle. For all the jobs, one tool: the fence pliers that were hammer and nippers and cutters and twisters and pry and vise and crimper and could open beer bottles, if you had them. Spring fence was simpler work than riding fence in the summer; the rattlers were denned up now, not cooling through the day in the rocks that shored up the fenceposts. It was tiresome, then, looking for them, hearing them, persuading them against their best instincts to leave the safe darkness and slither across open ground, where a hawk could pluck them up. And it was always persuasion with a stick a foot shorter than comfortable. They were more stupid than horses, belligerent, territorial, stubborn, and pitifully frightened, which made them dangerous. More than once she had dealt in a careful way with one and almost stepped on a second hidden in the same pile. One of Pete's Laws: Listen for the cavalry coming; it may be the other fella's.

She came over a roundback in sight of the ranch's entrance on the highway. A car was sitting in her road. It was a yellow Ford, full-size, four-door. She could see someone in it. She leaned back to the saddlebag and took out the little binoculars, the same kind she had given Benjy. Focus came up. She was looking at a man looking at her through a little pair of binoculars. He got out of his car. Slowly. He was a big man, with a big belly, big chest, big shoulders, and he moved on little dancer's legs in a slow, showy way.

He came around the Ford, spread his hands, and held them in a broad gesture. Through the glasses she could see that his hands were big too, see his iron-gray hair, cut short, open-collared button-down shirt, tailored khakis, windbreaker, running shoes with blue stripes. She could see a wolfish grin, amused at some part of the whole show they were making on the hills, as they warily kept their distance. She found herself abstracted by the glasses and the distance; he looked . . . like what? Like the roommate of a boy she went with in college, big, a center on the varsity team, who liked the confusion and violence at the middle of the scrimmage, a center who happened to be very bright but who seldom acknowledged that part of himself and stressed the violence, who had the same animal, cynical, knowing grin and grinned openly, knowingly at Cookie when she came to their room, knowing that she wanted sex, showing that he knew it with only the smile and no joke behind it, inviting her to play with someone who knew what it was like at the core of things whenever she was ready and that he was in no hurry. It had made her angry at the time, either at the wolfish center or at the boy she was dating, who didn't sense the subtext of looks and grins. She never did go to play with the center. She was angry with him for knowing. Perhaps now it wouldn't matter.

The big man dropped his hands. He reached around behind him, slowly, and brought out a gun. A Browning automatic. A man with big hands could use one. He held it above his head by the muzzle, displaying its presence. Mockingly, he opened the car door and bent inside. Cookie walked Rambler to the left so she could follow him. He put the Browning in the glove compartment, closed it, closed the car door, and displayed his hands. Nothing dangerous, his snide grin seemed to say, you can stop being afraid now. Against Pete's rules, she walked Rambler toward him, at least as far as talking distance but not

49

farther than the range of a rushed pistol shot. She stayed on the horse.

"Miss Culler." He grinned, emphasizing the "miss."

"You're on my land. Like to introduce yourself?"

"Do you have a favorite name?"

"Are we going to stand out here in the wind and trade snappy patter, or are you going to tell me who the fuck you are and why you put your fat ass on my land? I'm not having a great day here."

"The reason I ask about the name is that mine is kind of a sissy name, and I wouldn't want you to get the wrong impression of me. I'm sensitive."

"You look it."

"Well, I am." The grin was even wider and maybe sharper.

"Try me with the real one, and if I can't stand it we'll work on another."

"Miss Culler, meet Mr. Francis Fulton Xavier Coyne."

"Sounds Armenian."

"This"—he gestured around him dramatically—"is all yours?"

"No. Across the highway, up which the sheriff is due to come presently, is open range. Everything you see behind me is mine. Everything—everything on it, everything under it. You're on it, I don't own you, so maybe you better get off it."

"Miss Culler, I'm enjoying looking at you and your empire. You're a handsome woman. I'd like to see how you look in a dress, without a horse under you."

"You know, Mr. Coyne, a lot of older folks, mostly men, say that to me. They're usually disappointed." She walked Rambler to the side and slightly closer, so they didn't have to talk so loudly. She should have brought her S & W; she felt uncomfortable without it now, even though she knew this Boston mick—his vowels were stretched to that pattern— wasn't going to do anything so near the highway. It would

50

have given her some edge, is all.

"But enough chitchat, Mr. Coyne. Do you have business with me?"

He turned his face and looked at her sideways, grinning. You know I do, it said.

She ignored it. She wanted him to open something. Show me your hand, Francis, a flush or a straight. "I'm going. I have work to do, Mr. Coyne. You can send me roses and a cute poem about dresses and such from town."

"We do have business. We both know that. I have been asked to retrieve . . . data that belongs to others. When I have the data I will be gone, and you can go back to your work unimpeded. I have been most vigorously encouraged to press this with all my resources, which are considerable. Considerable, Miss Culler. May I call you Cookie?"

"I think I'd prefer that you address me more formally, Mr. Coyne. We're not friends."

"Yes, but we could be. There is no difficulty here. Yet. There's a misunderstanding that can be negotiated simply. Data, a location, a willingness to cooperate. I will press this. You know that, don't you?"

She looked at him. She knew it. He enjoyed his work. Everything he said, every movement he made, was mocking, toying, yet there was a palpable aura of power and heat around him. She realized that he was not like the center at all. The center was a boy. Francis Coyne could not be ignored.

"I'll tell you something," she said, leaning forward and resting her crossed forearms on the pommel of her saddle. "No one will hurt my brother. You may be a big man, Francis, but if you try to hurt him I will kill you. Like I'd kill a snake. You've sent one person to get him already, and that didn't work. You can pick him up at the hospital in about a week, I suspect. You, Francis, I'd have to kill. And I would."

51

"Unpleasant and foolish talk, Miss Culler. I didn't send anyone to harm your brother, and this can all be worked out. You think about it, and you will know that you must work it out. As I understand this situation, there is too much at stake to drop it. I will press until there is a resolution." The grin was still in place, but the eyes were serious now, and he lengthened his Boston vowels even longer, stressing each word.

"You think about it. You can reach me in town, at the motel, or you can just call my name, even softly, and chances are"— he was mocking again—"I'll be right there behind you."

"Don't do it, Francis. This isn't Boston Common. This is my place."

The whine of snow tires on dry pavement came over the rise, and Vern's four-by appeared like a toy half a mile west. Coyne turned to follow her look. "Your friend," he said. "Your father was a lawman, wasn't he?"

"You know quite a lot about me for a Bostonian, Mr. Coyne."

"A coffee shop in a small town, it's easy to learn a lot. People like to talk to a man who likes to talk at breakfast. I know all sorts of things about you and your father. I know all sorts of things about the mailman and about the barber too, but it's you who interest me. There's information all around for the asking. Why aren't you married, Miss Culler?"

"Am I supposed to be shocked by the sudden personal question?"

"No, not at all. Meeting you, I am genuinely puzzled."

"I snore."

"A pity."

The Blazer turned into the road and stopped beside Coyne's Ford. Vern got out and walked around to the fence.

"Cookie. Howdy." He grinned and said to the stranger, "I'm Vern McKillip."

"Ask him to vote for you, Vern. But you'd have to bend the rules. This is Mr. Francis Fulton Xavier Coyne, of Boston."

Vern reached across the fence and shook hands, the fourth-grade grin and the wolf's grin meeting.

"Mr. Coyne has a big old automatic pistol in the glove compartment of his car. He was waving it around a while back."

Vern frowned. "That so, Mr. Coyne?"

"I couldn't say," Coyne replied.

"Oh, it's there, all right, and there should be some kind of holster around behind Mr. Coyne's bulk there."

This was Vern's official grin now, the one he used being polite while issuing tickets or telling people to move on out of town. "Mr. Coyne, are you carrying a concealed weapon in my town?"

"Do you have reason to believe I am engaged in a harmful or felonious activity, Sheriff McKillip?"

"I just like to know about these things. Now let's take a look at that piece Cookie says you've got in your glove compartment."

"Not to be uncooperative, Sheriff, but if there were a handgun in the car it would almost undoubtedly be accompanied by a carry permit. I am a thorough man. You would probably find that I am a bonded messenger who must transport valuable goods and large sums of money. The gun would be legal and registered. But unless you have all the indications laid down by law, I would not insist on going through my car. Harassment, unlawful search: it would be a matter of principle to me to press"—he looked to Cookie as he stressed the word—"my legal rights."

"You a lawyer too, Mr. Coyne?"

"Yes. Massachusetts bar."

"Well, that's dandy, but I'm not sure I care for this situation of folks running around carrying pieces into the tavern and such. It's just bad control on my part, Mr. Coyne. And what have you got to hide from me? I'm the sheriff of a tiny little piece of country."

"You're right, Sheriff McKillip. This is not a healthy start. Miss Culler and I have just concluded our business. Why don't I call on you in your office later today and present my credentials and so forth?"

"That would be dandy, Mr. Coyne. I believe that's what you should have done in the first place, isn't it? Isn't there some obligation to check in with local officials when you bring your carry permit in?"

"A courtesy. Which I'll observe this afternoon. Sheriff. Miss Culler. Consider my offer, Miss Culler." He ducked through the fence, passed Vern, and walked around to his car door with the same exaggerated step, and grinning at her once again, he got in, started the car, and drove away. They watched until his car was a toy, as Vern's had been, until it disappeared over the last rise.

"What in hell is happening out here, Cookie?" Vern sounded put out that she would disturb the simplicity of his job. They were sitting in his Blazer; Rambler was grazing near the fence, with his girth loosened. "Nathan says you've got a boy that needs a ride to the hospital, that you'll explain it all, and now this Coyne fella. Is this all going to be a simple explanation? Am I going to understand this the first time? It's been a long time since I had to understand anything complicated." He shook his head and poured himself a cup of coffee from a thermos.

She took the cup from him and drank some of the strong coffee. "Mm. Real stuff. Bad for a man your age, Vern. The caffeine. Want to keep you around."

"You and Darlene. Caffeine, cigarettes, booze. Now what in hell is going on?"

54

She looked out at the highway, at the moving, muddled clouds.

"Cookie?"

"Vern. I've got to ask you to separate some ideas here. I need help from the law, and I need help from you. I want the good part of the law, and I don't want the bad part. If we were in Seattle or Boston or even Ellensburg, we'd have to take them both. But I've got you, and this is our town. I need you to listen to some things as the sheriff and some things as Vern, who used to sled down Risher's Run with me. I need you, Vern."

She didn't like to need anything. He could see the effort. He tried to make it easy on her. "I've known you all your life, all mine. I love you, Cookie. The law's important to me, but it's not family. It was important to Pete, but he knew there were some situations it didn't cover. If you tell me something, well, it's me. If you want me to do something, then that's law."

She nodded. Watched the clouds. He waited.

"Benjy's got into some trouble." Vern winced; he'd known Benjy a long time too. "Down south; Arizona. He flew a shipment of dope." Another wince, a look away. "He crashed, the shipment was burned, the people who bankrolled it and arranged it think some of it is left and want the location of the wreck, then they want Benjy dead."

"Lordy."

"They sent some little gunsel this morning. Nathan clipped him. With a damned skillet; broke his nose and cheekbone and maybe his jaw, it looks like. He should get to a doctor, but I don't want Benjy brought into it. This Coyne fella, I don't know exactly how he fits in, but the bankrollers sent him too. It's not the mob; just a bunch of amateur hoods. Benjy says they're dentists from West Virginia trying to make drug profits.

55

"I don't know what to do yet, but I want that little sonofabitch who came this morning put away. Attended to but put away. I'm beginning to get an idea, but I've got to spend the afternoon working it out."

"Where's Benjy now?"

"Up in the little valley, with Wilfred. I need the boy attended to, and I need some space, and I need to be able to call you and know you'll come on the run."

"I don't like your being up here alone, Cookie."

"I'm not alone. I've got Nathan and Willard and Bert and Wilfred and Benjy."

"Some army of desperadoes. Maybe I'll—"

"You just stay down there with Darlene and watch for me. If you see anybody strange, then call me. I've got to figure this out. I've got to go. Can you get that boy and take him into Ellensburg?"

"Sure. I can work up some kind of a charge that will keep him off the street. Maybe he even has a record. We could get lucky and find it. Shit, we've got a computer; I might as well use it. I can keep Benjy out of this for a while, but . . ." He let it hang.

"I know, Vern. He's got to reckon up, somehow. I'll be thinking of that too."

She kissed him in a fairly sisterly fashion. But she bit his ear before she opened the door and jumped out. She tightened Rambler's girth and mounted. By the time she had reached the top of the hill, Vern's four-by had crossed Goldpan Creek and was smoking the gravel up to the ridge.

Cookie rode slowly, still inspecting fence, thinking. She crossed Goldpan Creek above the little bridge and stopped to let Rambler drink. Then up across the grazing land parallel to the road. Instead of crossing the ridge higher, by the horse trail that threaded through boulders, she angled down to a gate near the road. She and Rambler took the road up to the ridge, where it dropped off on one side and was overhung by boulders on the other. She stopped there for a time and continued down into the valley.

When she heard Vern's Blazer, she turned Rambler into the trees. She didn't want to see him just then. She didn't want to see anyone.

CHAPTER TEN

Nathan knew. They had been together, off and on, for six years. Add to that his talent for nurturing. He could feel and distinguish needs the way a wine taster could read the scents in a claret. Cookie's needs were not complex, and they became as plain to him as the smell of wood smoke in the air. Sometimes she needed warmth, sometimes space, sometimes she needed freedom and at other times attention. At her lowest she needed sensation, sharp peaks for all her senses, to center her again, bring her back to her own body and set her working on her own active terms. She confronted the world with her body, tasted it, slapped it on the back, sniffed its crotch, listened to its tappets. She immersed herself in it and used the rush of action to sort the small stuff out. When Cookie was low, it was because she had lost her momentum, she was outside her senses and her advantages. She needed to sink back into herself. He could help there.

She rubbed down and curried Rambler and gave him a treat, two apples from the feed room. Red worked all day because he loved it, but Rambler would get peevish without treats. She gave Red an apple anyway. He seemed puzzled but accepted it.

The front door, for some damned reason, was locked. Cookie banged on it a few times—"Shit, goddamned city boy"—and walked around back. Here, the reason was apparent. He had filled the hot tub and fired the stove that sat in it. The flue was smoking like a cartoon locomotive, and the water steamed in the early-evening air. Her terry-cloth robe hung from a branch near the flue, where it would be warm. A glass pitcher of Manhattans sat on the shelf that was braced against the side of the tub, with a short crystal tumbler, an oil lamp gleaming softly in the dusk, two books, and four small bowls. They held salted almonds, tiny sour cornichons, bittersweet miniature chocolates, half a dozen early wildflower blossoms. A wicker basket sat beside the step to the tub's lip, and when she approached it she could smell the herb and petal potpourri he had sprinkled on the surface of the tub.

She sat on the step and didn't move for a minute or more, watching the sunset change and fade on the clouds that had broken just before sunset, then she took her boots and socks off. She stood and peeled away her Levi's and her panties, and dropped them in the basket beside her, then her shirts and the silk chemise under them, standing naked in the cool, letting it touch her skin.

The wood deck was chill under her bare feet. She turned on the shower head that was bracketed to the outside wall. The drum of the water on the wood sounded like summer. The water was warm, soaking her all over. A new bar of Swedish soap, smelling like balsam, was in the dish that sat on a sill. She stepped out of the water rush and soaped herself with slick fragrance. She rinsed. Under the rush of water, part of the starch she had used to oppose the day's trouble dissolved. She was weary and wanted a drink.

Slowly, she lowered herself into the tub, accepting the heat, which seared, then softened, the tightness of her muscles. She was all the way in. The pitcher made a musical clink against the glass, and the Manhattan she lifted to her mouth smelled of rye and vermouth, a wild distilled fragrance. The nuts and cornichons were point counterpoint, and both made the Manhattan taste sweeter. Then she tried a chocolate, as small as a wild cherry, deep bittersweet with a moist bead of hazelnut truffle within it. It brought out the herb taste of the vermouth. It also lingered on her tongue and mixed with the taste of rye. There was a book of Roman poetry, and Anaïs Nin's *Delta of Venus.* In twenty minutes she had sipped two Manhattans and felt, finally, the heat meet at her core, penetrating every part of her, leaving her al dente or even, for pasta, slightly overcooked.

The robe was warm. Her sheepskin slippers were there. She left the clothes but carried in the boots with the last of the Manhattans.

Nathan was wearing a silk robe. He put down his glass as she came in. "Nathan . . ." she started, in thanks, but he stepped quickly to her and put his hand to her mouth.

He shook his head. "No words . . ." he said.

She nodded, began to turn, to bustle the boots and the Manhattan away, but he took them and put them on the floor against the wall and stood to her again immediately. She was puzzled. He didn't kiss her, didn't hug her. She reached for him, and he shook his head. No, not yet, it said.

The stove by the bed, a Defiant wood stove, was open, with a fire going, the radiant glow on her cheek. Nathan stood her at the foot of the bed and took a cloth from his pocket, a large silk handkerchief. He folded it diagonally and then in bars, so it made a long, flat band with pointed ends. He kissed her, once on each cheek, and laid the silk against her eyes, tying it behind her head. She could see nothing. She could hear the crackle of the fire. She could smell the drink he had put down, juniper, a martini.

He undid her robe and lifted it away from her. The fire was warm. His hand came up behind the small of her back and her shoulder blades, and he tilted her back, holding her, assuring

61

her with his strong hands, until she lay on the bed. Her slippers were taken from her feet. He moved quietly, but she could hear the faint purr of his silk robe.

His hands turned her over on her stomach. A new smell. Coconut. Ouch! Cold, something cold drizzled on her shoulders, down her spine. The bed moved; he was beside her, his hands on her back. It was massage oil, and his hands kneaded her muscles, rolled them over the bones beneath, pressed them away from their attachments, gathered them back. Her shoulders, her neck far up around her ears, the small of her back, her nates, until they had new shape, new identity. Her legs, the big thigh muscles. She wanted to crush his hips inside them, to have them locked around his face. Between, between! Delicately around her knees, feeling for the flesh that filigreed the bone. Then the calves, the long bouncing muscles, the ankles, his hands gripping but gentle. The feet, her roots, her supple toes, her soft pads which felt every touch so exquisitely. What was he doing? He turned and bent and flexed her feet with his hands until they were hardly her own. Now, she pleaded, reach up for me now.

But he would not.

Instead he took, suddenly, chillingly, delightfully, her long first toe into his mouth, sucking it, circling it with his tongue, using it to fuck his mouth, sucking in and out. Prickles of excitement ran over her. One toe, then another, and when he left a toe, the moisture of his saliva was cool.

What was he doing? He turned her over, spread her legs. Take me right now, reach into me, but he would not.

A new smell. Orange? His hand was close to her face, fragrant of orange, his finger near her mouth. She eagerly sucked it in, come in, come in. The bite of alcohol, Cointreau, oranges. She sucked it all and his finger went away. Another cool assault, the same smell, now, thank God, on her breasts. He rubbed Cointreau from his finger to her nipples. Oh,

62

quickly, she begged, come to them quickly. His mouth closed over one as the other stiffened with the chill of evaporating alcohol. Yes, she begged, suck it dry. Now the other, rougher with this nipple, kneading the breast with his hand, using his teeth lightly. Yes, bite me, suck me hard. No, don't stop, don't leave. His mouth at her mouth, she opened to him and felt the warm flood of brandy now, as their tongues steeped and swirled in it. More, she begged. More now. His hands worked at her breasts as he kissed her again: Amaretto. Delicious, he's delicious. Give me your cock, dip it in chocolate, in bourbon, in cream, in butterscotch, give it to me, but he would not.

He parted her legs. She felt his weight on the bed between them. His breath was heavy and warm against her thighs, his hands fondled her bush, pulled it back to open her, oh! The first touch of his tongue was like a shock, and then another, and then they came together as he rooted into her like a truffle swine, noisily and hungrily wanting her scent and her saline sweetness, coming upon the jewel and staying. She had both her hands in his hair now, hoping she wasn't hurting him but not caring, pulling his frantic mouth into her cunt, rising now, her whole body floating. Her own shaking breath fluttering with images of roads, lakes, trees rushing at her like trains, teeth clenched until they hurt, beautifully, fingers clutching his black, black, black hair, rising high, flooding, here it comes, oh no, please no, please yes, please, please, please, and she screamed softly, crying, weeping into the blackness of the silk as her palpitating soul drained into his tongue.

It came and passed and came again, waves, spasms, freshets, storms and showers of pleasure, and all she wanted now was him inside her. Weeping, she pulled him to her, tearing the blindfold aside, pulling at his shoulders, hands on his face as she bent up to kiss him hard, hands on his hips as she guided him, reaching down to feel his cock slip into her, one finger following it deliriously to feel it go in and out against her softness, hands on his tight ass, knees up around his ass, deeper, oh you bastard, much deeper, all deep, all inside. And he bucked and plunged and shuddered and she was with him, holding him for pity's sake, then feeling him small sweetly, and just as his depleted cock slipped out they were both, needfully, finally, asleep. Cookie was centered.

CHAPTER ELEVEN

When Cookie came out the front door, she had found her old grin. You devil, she thought. And she was moving fast. She had an idea now, and she would move with it. It wasn't all worked out, but the parts would fall into place as she jostled it. She had a notebook, a coffee cup, and a lumpy canvas tote. Nathan's store list was in it, four dozen eggs from her chickens, and her .41 magnum. She dropped everything but the coffee and her checkbook in her pickup.

The bunkhouse was across the barnyard, about forty yards. Bert and Willard were already gone, damn. But she heard noises from the tractor shed. Closer, she could hear both of them.

"Je-sus, Willard." Bert's voice was nasal and high-pitched, with a space between each word. "You are going to ruint that fine piece of machinery, swiping away at it with a file as would scrape the nose off a elk." Bert was tall and spare, older, something over sixty. He wore thick glasses with plastic-and-metal frames and was never seen without a hat over his apparently bald pate.

"Will you please just shut the billy-fuck up, will you? I am the only one arount here who cares that these goddamned pisspot machines run regular. Certain sure not you, who couldn't flush a toilet without the destructions." Willard was a tiny man with mincing gestures, excitable, beetle-browed, with fine reddish hair piled up with spray into a country-music DJ pompadour.

"Hey, troops."

"Cookie, Willard here is bejabbering our power takeoff on that old Cub tractor, trying to cornhole it with a rasp file, and you just try, I say try, to get parts for that little sucker in this day and age."

"Bert, you are talking out of your own puckered hole. Shit, shit; all the shit I hear from you about what you don't know nothing from. Look at that." He waved the file under Bert's glasses. "That look like a goddamned rasp file? A rasp file, you old sheep-queer, has little-bitty teeth sticking up all along it. Find a tooth number one on there, I stand and de-fy you to find one. Cee-fucking-reist, you are as dense as a man breathing can be." He was disgusted.

"Fact remains, Willard, you are taking away metal that we aren't getting back, not in this lifetime." He was maddeningly reasonable.

The Bert and Willard show. A card table with Bert and Willard and Wilson and Father Gogarty around it was dangerous for a man with asthma; he could die laughing.

"Well, leave off fucking the machinery for a minute there, Willard," Cookie said. "We got some figuring to do." They walked into the sun and hunkered down with their backs to the shed wall, three in a row.

"Boys, I've got to be straight with you. And I know you'll keep what I'm telling you here on the ranch." She needn't have said it, wouldn't have if she weren't worried about it. They knew that and nodded, looking off toward the mountain face. "Got some trouble with friends of Benjy's. He's back, he's made some eastern types real angry, and they may try and get him. Hell, one tried already."

"Fuck. Let 'em try again," said Willard, like a bantam rooster.

"Willard, some of these fellas are mean types, real pros. That's my concern, that you two don't get hurt. Best you not get involved in this. This is something family, and I don't mean to mix anybody up in it. Now, I tell you what: I'll write out a check for your wages through this month and the next. You leave me six mounts and drive the stock over to Jimpson's, bunk out there until this is over. Probably a couple weeks."

Willard fidgeted for a moment, then rose quickly and stalked into the shed. Rasping and banging began almost immediately. Cookie said, "Well, shit, what's with him?"

Bert didn't speak right away and didn't look at her. "Cookie," he said, in his long-nosed twang, softly, "I've knowed you twenty years, more. I got about fifteen or twenty years on you for age, too, so I'll say this to you as your friend and not your hand. You've hurt Willard, there. You've told him he's not family and not worth risking and probably not a good man when the chips come down. I don't think you meant to. You don't have a speck of mean in you, Cookie. But you better get up and walk right in there and apologize to that man. He'd eat nails for you. As for me, I wasn't going to go anyway, so it doesn't matter."

They both looked at the mountain for a moment more, then Cookie looked at Bert, his thin face lined from squinting out the sun and wind, and stubbled with Monday's beard. She leaned over and kissed his stubbly cheek. He smiled at the mountain and she got up. "Willard," she called, "stop fucking over that machinery and listen to me. I've said a stupid thing."

She knew it would come to her piece by piece, and this was one of the pieces, just as her foot went up into the pickup. She closed the door and walked to the ranch house. "Laven-

67

stein," she called, "get out here, you sexy thing."

He appeared in the doorway, reading a sheaf of photocopies. "Mm?" He was unnerving that way; he could be the most attentive and passionate lover, then get out of bed and continue at the same page in his research, whatever that was. It was his way of distancing, and with Cookie, it may have been necessary.

"Lavenstein, look." She took the photocopies from his hand over his protests and began drawing on the back of one with his pencil. "Look, here's the ridge, north and south. It ends here, at the gully, a drop-off. Here's Goldpan Creek, the bridge, the road out, and the highway. There. This little cross, that's where we wore down the grass fucking last summer. Okay. Dotted line, the horse trail over the ridge, through boulders—these little round things. Good, huh? More geography, Lavenstein: Souk River and the valley, wet fields south, wet fields north. Right. Here we are, here's Wilfred and Benjy up on the mountain face. Done. Look at this, Nathan. The road. It's the only road to us."

"Seems to be. Point?"

"What you do for whoever you do it for—you blow up things, right?"

"Not directly. Not even indirectly. But go ahead."

"Could you tell me how much dynamite to close the road where the rock hangs over it? And how much to blow the bridge? Do we blow the goddamned bridge?"

"What good would that do?"

"Did you notice the shoes on that kid you had lunch with? Little Eye-talian numbers. Cut this road"—she put a line through the road where it touched the ridge and the gully— "and they're out of their element. They're on foot in my backyard."

Nathan looked at the drawing.

"Can you figure out things like that or just how to zap rockets, Jewboy?"

68

He thought a moment more. "What percentage blasting gelatin can you buy?"

Wilson and Charlie were just about to attack their lunch, and the Lionel train was making full steam past the kitchen door, hooting like a mechanical owl.

"Weeelson. Charlie, how are you, you old hermit?"

"Hey, Cookie," Charlie said, a big, shy man, young, behind thick glasses.

"Cookie, you sweet morsel, have a bite of my lunch, and then I'll have a bite of you, my savage empress."

"Thanks." Her mouth was already full of his taco. "Need some help . . . and . . . napkin." She threw up her hand to Sanchez, three fingers up. When the Coronas arrived, she started at the beginning and explained.

Father Gogarty was on his knees in the backyard of the parish house, talking to himself, declaiming, making points, making finger holes in the turned earth.

"You're planting those too early. Winter's not over," she said.

"Faith," he said. "I have faith." Gogarty talked to himself all the time, about all his parishioners, about everything. He was accustomed to being discovered rattling on about something. He turned and smiled at her. He appreciated Cookie in the theoretical way a celibate can—with effort—look carefully at a woman with broad, muscular hips and good boobs. She was good for him, he had concluded; she kept his vows fresh and gave his confessor something to hear.

Cookie liked Gogarty. He was thirty-five, good-looking, spoken for, but in a way unlike Vern's commitment to Darlene. She always felt his eyes on her, pleasant, and felt the respect too. Also pleasant. The titillation of being ravished by a prayer-crazed hermit monk passed through her mind. She smiled wider, that high-wattage Cookie smile that couldn't hide anything. She always lost money at poker. "Faith in what, Gogarty?"

He picked up the little envelopes and peered at the small print. "In the seed envelopes," he replied. It was a good pulpit voice, a better singing voice at "Roddy McCorley," and had broad vowels with the inflectional lilt of a first-generation family whose parents still argued in Gaelic. "Early April, darlin'—look there." He handed her a packet.

"That's for Rhode Island or Georgia or someplace where the winter commutes on schedule, Gogarty."

"Mm. God needs city boys too," he decided. "Saint Francis was, essentially, a city boy, you know."

"Didn't know. Gogarty, how many cops in your family?"

"Cookie, you must dissuade yourself from thinking in stereotypes. I'm from a large eastern city—"

"Not Atlanta."

"Very well, I am from Boston, and my family is of Irish extraction. Priests, nuns, and police are not the only things the Irish aspire to, my child." He was still poking holes in the earth with his index finger. "We breed poets and engineers too."

"How many cops?"

"Two brothers, one sister. John, detective first grade. Larry, desk sergeant. And Mary Elizabeth, our baby, is taking her sergeant's exam next month; we have the greatest hopes."

"I need some information about a Boston fella. All the information I can get won't be too much, and it could be the kind that your family can give me."

He had heard too many confessions to ask, What for? He just poked another few holes and she volunteered it.

"It's a story for a case of beer and a windy night, but it goes like this in the short form: My brother's in trouble with some rough guys from back there. He probably bought into it, but

70

I'm not letting him get hurt. One fella came with a gun, and he's in the hospital. Another fella, he's different. I don't have him figured yet. He's maybe more dangerous because he's smarter, been around. Boston fella. Name of Francis Fulton Xavier Coyne. With a name like that, I figured he was one of your boys. Says he's a lawyer, but he carries an automatic under his jacket."

"That's more merciful than most lawyers," Gogarty said.

"It would be good to know what I'm dealing with," she said.

"How about Vern?"

"Well, Gogarty, he's hanging around the edges of this thing, but I've got to think of Benjy. Try to get him squared away without the law being heavy-handed."

"Cookie, someone has to be heavy-handed with Benjy sometime. You won't be. He's got to answer for things. You've bailed him out too many times. You're manufacturing a cripple there. You're aiding and abetting from a distance."

"He's a good boy, Gogarty. If you'd only known him before he left the ranch. And he feels bad about all this, I know he does."

Gogarty shook his head and poked the earth. "There's good in the boy, though he really shouldn't be so much a boy at his age. You lend him too much of your own good, Cookie. And while we're speaking philosophically . . ."

"What's that, Faddah?" she asked, giving her best Dead End Kids imitation.

"Nothing. Let me plant my mustard seeds of faith." He looked at the packets. "Sixty cents isn't a steep wager on faith. I can always buy more. I'll call my family this evening."

"Thanks, Gogarty." She leaned down, punched him in the arm, and was gone.

He was going to say something, something meddlesome about the comfort of having a partner. He was going to say

71

something about Vern McKillip and Darlene, and Nathan Lavenstein and Cookie. Something about Cookie's trips to Seattle, and about things that happened years before. . . . It was his job, after all. And she was his friend. He knew a few things about Cookie almost no one did. He spoke to the holes in the earth about her, talking to himself again.

CHAPTER TWELVE

She locked her doors. She could hardly remember how to do it. She'd never locked the doors of her pickup before. But the little cardboard carton on the floor seemed heavier than it was, and it sat with suspicious silence; such a carton ought to make some noise, like a rattlesnake that hears your footsteps through the ground and warns you off. She covered it with a tarp before she left, and she didn't know whether she was locking people out or locking the dense little gray packets in.

She'd left eggs for Gogarty and for Millie (the shirt was almost done). She'd given a dozen to Wilson and Charlie, and brought the last dozen into Mr. McGregor's. The lights were dim; the afternoon drinkers looked suitably dissipated in the glow from Coors neon and Budweiser bubble signs and the lighted panels under the rows of bottles. The smell of spilled beer and cigarette smoke reminded her of Pete. She'd sat at his knee in a hundred places like this, with fewer ferns and no salad bar, and listened with him as a story was unrolled, embellished, revised, and played out for them. Pete would tell a story, not at first but later, about law days, or early days coming through the passes, when there was just a two-lane and no snow roofs, or hunting in big parties. Cookie, just big enough to reach and read the selections on the jukebox, would tell stories about horses she had almost ridden, cats that had scratched her, right here, or when she had seen a hawk fly down and grab one of her chickens, bang, like that. Lawmen and hard cases and afternoon drinkers and bartenders listened quietly, with their full attention, and commented seriously, empathetically, on the unpredictability of cats and horses and, absolutely, hawks. She had grown up around places like this; they were a kind of public living room for Pete and Cookie. She could not remember her mother coming with them. She knew but could not remember, because it was ingrained as an attitude rather than a code, the etiquette of storytelling, more rigorous and less plain than which fork to use. She also came to recognize tensions that twisted the air around a table when certain men met certain men: bad blood, old angers. Or simply dangerous men.

"Tom," she called, out of reverie and back in full voice, about like a truck scraping a guardrail, "hen eggs from the girls."

Tom smiled, nodded thanks, and pointed to her booth.

"I'll try a Dos Equis and some salsa, Tom." A few minutes later, she picked up the long-necked bottle with her little finger and the bowls of chips and salsa in either hand, so she stood with her hands full as Francis Fulton Xavier Coyne rose politely, or mockingly, at her approach.

"Mr. Coyne, you're in my booth."

"Miss Culler, I know."

He is a strange man, she thought. He was dressed today in a tweed suit and looked more like professorial tenure than professional extortion. It was probably woven in Donegal, she thought, by Coynes. He smiled at her, that smile that knew something bitterly, secretly funny, and they stood there until her little finger was tired.

Shake hands with the devil, Pete had said; he plays a good hand of poker. "Sit yourself down, Mr. Coyne," she said, "and tell me how things are on the other side of the soul business."

"After you, Miss Culler."

His mama had taught him. She was not accustomed to manners. She didn't know if she liked them. But she sat.

She lifted her beer. "Will you have a drink, Mr. Coyne?"

"I have one, thank you." He lifted his glass. "We had a bad beginning. Here's to a new understanding."

She didn't reply but looked closely at him, frowning in concentration, as she drank from her bottle.

"Hey! Hey, Cookie! Say hey, Cooks, how about a drink?"

She looked up at P.J. Hambling. Oh, Lord, this will be sticky. It was only with drunks that she regretted her loose ways. Other old lovers became good friends; that's the way she worked it, a trade of friendship for her independence. It didn't work with drunks. "P.J., you old bulldogger. You look a little worse for wear, old son. Best you get flat somewhere."

"Sure, Cooks. I like the idea. Drink first, we get flat later. Good idea." He turned to Coyne. "Cookie's always got the best damn ideas. How about you? Tom," he shouted over his shoulder, "let's have a drink for this sumbitch. What you want?"

"I have a drink," Coyne said pleasantly.

P.J. looked at it, squinted his eyes. "You sure?" He picked up Coyne's glass and sniffed it noisily. "Shit," he said, using two long syllables, "there's no drink in that drink. I'm buying you a real drink."

Cookie was worried. Coyne showed no sign of annoyance, but P.J. could be dangerous. He'd been a first-class rodeo athlete before Jack Daniel started getting better scores than he did. She also knew that P.J. laid the drunk act on heavier than he felt it; it let him get away with some bad behavior and a lot of angry talk. Maybe he needed that.

"Come on, what you want? Don't have all day. Cookie and I wanta take our nap."

"Thank you . . ." Coyne looked at Cookie for reference. "P.J.? Thank you, P.J., but I have this little sissy drink."

"Get you a man's drink, horse."

"Can't, P.J. I'm an alcoholic."

"Shit. You don't look drunk to me."

"I'm not. But I can't drink. Alcohol's a poison to me. I drink, and I go around making scenes in bars. I get embarrassed for myself."

P.J. eyed him, squinting again. "Sissy drink. You a sissy, huh? You one of them eastern seaboard pussyboys?"

Coyne nodded. "I'm wearing lacy pink shorts under this suit, right now."

"Shit," P.J. said, and stopped, puzzled. He walked away, gesturing back at Coyne with his thumb for the bar crowd. "Eastern pussyboy."

"Are you really?" Cookie asked.

"Wearing pink shorts?"

"An alcoholic."

Coyne picked up his soda water in a toast. "I am," he said, "and five years sober."

She was angry, suddenly. She could understand a hoodlum coming after Benjy, someone she could despise as small and vile, but she couldn't understand this man coming after him. "Just what the fuck are you here for, Coyne, and why are we sitting here drinking whatever we're drinking, and where do you get off coming for my brother? Get the hell out of here before you get hurt. I swear you *will* get hurt. What the fuck are you up to?" She should keep her voice down just this once. The air was beginning to have that old tense feeling.

"Please, Miss Culler. I didn't come here to harm your brother. I was sent to get information; it's what I'm good at. Sometimes I have to get it from unpleasant people, sometimes I work for people who are unpleasant, but I am good at my work."

"Then why did you send that kid with the gun?"

"I sent no one. It is possible that my employers sent someone, although I don't know why."

"Just who are your employers?"

"Amateurs, Miss Culler. They have never been in situations with rocks and hard places on both sides, and the only set of options they know are the ones they've learned from TV. Not a very practical school of instruction. It makes them unpredictable. And dangerous.

"I am not trying to intimidate or frighten. I want one thing only. The location of a crash site. My employers may want more, but I will dissuade them. If I have assurances from you and your brother that he won't pressure them in return. We can negotiate a stalemate here, Miss Culler."

She looked at him, understanding even less what he might be.

"Hey! Pussyboy!"

Certainly not that.

P.J. and two of his barstool compañeros came to the booth. Coyne put his drink down.

P.J. began to mince back and forth in front of them, enjoying the attention of the bar, putting on his fairy act. "Oh, where will I get me a date for the ball? Where's the pussyboy of my dreams?" P.J. discovered Coyne. "Girls, look at this. Isn't he just delicious? He's my one and only prince. Say, Mr. Prince, you better go home and get dressed real pretty for the ball, don't you think?"

Cookie didn't like this. P.J.'s baiting was no more of a burden than any drunk's malicious psychodrama, but Coyne's lack of reaction truly frightened her. He smiled. A new, twisted smile that didn't involve his eyes; they were eager, interested, but cold. His hands lay flat and still on the tabletop.

"Come on, Mr. Prince." P.J. was done with mincing. "Time to go get your gown." P.J. reached over, with his friends, and

77

grabbed Coyne. Coyne's smile didn't change. "Get up and out the door, pussyboy, or you're gonna be hurtin' soon, hurtin' serioso."

They had him on his feet. Cookie started to rise. "God damn it, P.J., you crazy drunk . . ."

"Keep out of this, Cookie. We'll take care of this." They were hustling Coyne across the room, past the bar. Tom was protesting, but the few still at the bar were into the fun now, fat pussyboy getting the rush. She caught a glimpse of Coyne's face, still smiling, saying nothing. He was allowing himself to be thrown out, to be frogwalked, jostled, kicked, and spun out the door by a burnt-out rodeo rider and two haydrivers. She was confused. Nothing she had learned about Coyne helped her understand this. He was gone.

P.J. came back to her table with his band of desperados. "Hey, Cookie! Took care of him for ya. Listen, Cooks, ought not hang around shit like that. Bad for a fine-looking woman like you, and you are fine, Cooks."

"P.J., you shut your damn mouth. You little bar rat. Tom, a lowlife like this shouldn't be in here." She was angry; her face was red and her lips were tight. P.J. didn't know whether to get angry himself or to wallow a little in her attention, such as it was. "You got no sense, you got no manners, you got no respect, you got nothing, nothing but your old rodeo belt buckles. You got shit." She'd begun to get up, but that was when she noticed Coyne had come back in.

While P.J. pretended to laugh at her anger, she watched Coyne take off his tweed jacket and hang it carefully on the back of a chair beside the door. Tom saw him too, and was dialing the phone. Coyne took off his tie, a charcoal knit, and tucked it deftly into the jacket pocket. She was afraid of what would happen now, and was noticing small details as some people observe bits of reality during accidents.

P.J. saw her face change. For a moment he thought his

laughter had affected her, but he followed her eyes. Still chuckling, he turned and watched Coyne moving chairs aside, opening a space. He was no longer trapped in a booth; he had his threats arrayed before him and not around him. One of the desperado haydrivers reached for a knife he carried in his pocket and discovered it was no longer there. Coyne moved another chair, seemed to like the arrangement, and stood back to admire it. He rolled up one sleeve, then another, like a man about to do delicate work.

At least P.J. had never given up on a bronco; he had that much in him. He said, "What you want, pussyboy?"

Coyne looked at the three of them, appraisingly, and pointed to the one who had lost his knife. "Him. I want to give the greasy one a big kiss. The one who's lost his balls. The one who's about to wet his pants."

The haydriver flew at him with a plan: hit him once and get out the door behind him. He rushed at Coyne and drew back his fist as he came on, but Coyne, who seemed immovable, had stepped forward suddenly. The driver's rush stopped as a fist came out of nowhere and stabbed into his nose, his cocked fist unused in the air behind him.

Cookie watched as Coyne slipped his bulk to the right with those prancing little feet and legs, then kicked quickly side-ways. The haydriver's knee buckled the wrong way with a bad popping sound, and he went down.

P.J. and the other haydriver went for him together. But they were coming from the same side and got in each other's way. It was a moment of confusion, during which Coyne's toe kicked up between the haydriver's clenched fists and buried itself just under his rib cage and just over his stomach. The driver was down, trying to breathe again.

P.J. circled. Coyne circled back to the second driver, who was pulling himself into the dark, and took careful aim with one heel. He brought his weight and the force of a downward kick onto the back of the driver's right hand, and that was another bad sound that had small bones in it.

Coyne was still smiling. It was not an amused smile but almost contemplative, as if he were holding himself away from this and watching it. The old Korean man who had instructed him would have appreciated this smile, but it frightened Cookie. And fascinated her.

P.J. came on, an experienced bar fighter. He got in close, too close for kicking and that shit. He got close and grappled, tried to get his leg around behind the big man, get him down where his bulk might slow him, but, too quickly it seemed, they were going down, or P.J. was landing a body length away. His shirt was torn and he didn't know how it had happened, but he rolled and leaped up to one side. But Coyne wasn't coming after him. Coyne was waiting, smiling.

P.J. ran at Coyne, fists ready. Slam the side of his head and knock the fat sonofabitch down. Coyne moved, but he didn't move. He dipped to one side, like a dancer, and the force of P.J.'s rush was expended in throwing himself forward on the floor. Before P.J. could recover, Coyne's toe had broken in three of the ribs on his left side. P.J. rolled, the pain awful, but Coyne was there, over him, the heel of his hand slamming down on the bridge of his nose. So that's broken again, P.J. thought, a part of him still rational in the middle of things. He had been a good man, he knew it himself, a good roper and all-rounder, P.J. had; so he tried to rise, punch the sumbitch in the nuts, but Coyne danced again and, without a great effort, dislocated P.J.'s arm. P.J. passed out.

Cookie realized she had a bottle in her hand. She dropped it. It didn't break on the wooden floor but rolled, spitting beer, over against the second haydriver, who didn't notice the wetness spreading under him. He was concentrating on breathing. She looked at Coyne, wondering who, what he was. He was not smiling now. Now he was angry. In her

80

minute watching she saw his hands begin to shake and saw him control it. He could be a killer, but she was not sure he was. He was almost too rational. A vagrant thought came to her, Coyne as a young Jesuit, the order of the universe. She looked at him, beginning to sweat only now, drawing into himself, his brow closing in furrows. She walked to him. "Coyne," she said.

He looked at her. There was the merest image of a grin that passed his face, the only one she had seen that was not sharp, an embarrassed smile of recognition, but it was gone quickly. He shook his head; he couldn't talk now. He turned for his coat.

Vern was standing in the doorway with two deputies. He looked at the men on the floor and then at Cookie. She held her hands up and shrugged her shoulders. He looked at Tom. Tom shook his head, no complaints. Vern looked at Coyne and saw that he would not ask him any questions tonight.

"Mr. Coyne."

"Sheriff McKillip."

"Would it be convenient to stop by my office in the morning?"

Coyne nodded his head. He took his coat over his arm and walked to Tom, behind the bar. He took out a bill and laid it on the bar. "My apologies," he said.

Tom handed back the bill and said, "None needed, mister. Come again. Soda's on the house."

Coyne left, stepping over the first haydriver. When the door opened, Cookie could see that evening had come and that there was a light rain.

CHAPTER THIRTEEN

"Expanding gas," Lavenstein was saying, "not an explosion. Black powder was a poor blasting medium because it was an explosion. Zap." She did not appreciate the way he was handling the cylinders, the fat candles in gray paper wrapping, overprinted in three languages: Watch out, go away, be careful, this is the stuff that will blow your ass off. "A blasting medium chemically retards the explosion." He was pushing an awl into the end of one candle; she winced. "Spreads it out. The difference is shorter than the human span of perception, but it's the difference between zap and whoosh—controlled expansion of gas lifting and pushing."

"And blowing your ass off," Cookie said sourly, not wanting to be near the nasty little things.

"This is relatively safe stuff," Lavenstein said. "That's how Nobel made the money, making it safe."

"Relatively."

"Sure, you wouldn't want to subject this to too much shock. What you have is energy in an energy pocket; if you add enough energy to lift it out of its pocket, it releases everything. Bang."

"Whoosh. Just finish up with that stuff, Nathan. I'll use one as a dildo later. But not too energetically."

"Kinky."

"I've just disgusted myself. Finish up with that damn stuff."

He wrapped seven together with baling wire, twisting it tight with pliers. She could see how the wire bit softly into the sticks. "These," he said, respectfully, motioning to Willard, who approached from a distance and handed him a red plastic box, "these are the nasty little devils. These you don't mess with." He took one blasting cap out and held it lightly in his mouth while he closed the lid and handed it off to Willard. Willard retreated with elaborate nonchalance, pretending he didn't mind holding the box. Nathan pushed the blasting cap into the awl hole and looked the package over.

"This makes me dribble my drawers, Nathan. Scares me something fierce. How is it you fool with this stuff so easy?"

Nathan was leaning down into the rock cleft they had scraped and dug out, seeing how deep the package would go. "Do you know how many physics and chemistry students are killed every year in labs? When I was . . . at . . . Columbia, we had"—reaching, feeling in the black space within the rock—"one lab go, with six students and a full professor. Students are easy . . . to get, but . . . those full professors hurt." He pulled the package out again and motioned with his head for Bert, who brought over his shovel. "About three shovelfuls of that fine stuff on this side," he said, and Bert obliged him, as you or anyone else would oblige a man holding seven sticks of high explosive. Bert retreated. Nathan looked around, looked at the package again. "It's because we deal with pure stuff, trying not to mix our results. We fool with pure elements, very reactive, very elemental, if you will. It is not uncommon to see a block of pure sodium, which is an angry element on its own but docile enough when you salt your French fries. We work with fluoride, cyanide, with acids that would burn right through you and then eat the floor." He had checked the roll of wire beside him and was attaching two leads, red and yellow, to the wire leads that emerged from the blasting cap's copper crimp. "We want to isolate results. We want to separate ourselves from the gray, mixed, mongrel reactions of life and discover the principles behind them. Of course, I've also worked with shaped charges and high explosives in fieldwork, weapons testing, that sort of thing."

"Your work," she said. "You make weapons for the government, right?"

"I don't work for the government," he said, an edge just showing in his voice. "The Laboratory is an independent facility. We do pure science, as pure as science comes now. The application of our results is not our concern. For men of science it never has been possible to license application for good or bad. We investigate, they instigate."

Cookie looked at the coil of wire. "You guys have a long wire between you and the bomb, then. That's comfy."

"Don't philosophize, Cookie; it's not your long suit. Bert, Willard, let's pack the dirt over this charge pretty firmly—shovel and tamp."

Cookie got up and dusted off. The cars had been driven out to the bridge, supplies laid in; anything else would come over the ridge by . . . She was stung by Nathan's coolness. Who ran the damn ranch anyway? Nathan was just a dude on it. Didn't even like horses. There was some sense in that, Pete would agree, but where did he get off? She wanted him to come close and apologize with a hug, something. Would a little head be entirely out of the question? She joked with herself but she knew him too well; he could care for her in some extraordinary ways, but they were like his experiments, distant and under his own controls. Nathan didn't so much give as supply, and application was up to the grantee.

"Let's move back around the ridge, be sure we have everything," he was saying. "Bert and Willard, bring the tools; I'll lay down the wire. Cookie, you bring the rest of the carton."

85

He indicated the dynamite with his head. She hated the stuff. Maybe he knew it. "Willard, be careful with the caps."

It was like a car part with a crank for your hand, heavy and cold, as big as a can of beans. Nathan attached the leads to wing nuts on its side.

"Don't know why we've got to ruint a perfectly drivable road built at great labor by some of us when you was wrapped in diapers. Hell and damn, we could just park the damn tractor in the middle and then have the damned road when we wanted to bring in something that might be important, like parts or something. You ever think about these things?" Willard was offended by shutting off the road, but he was usually offended by something.

"Willard," Bert began, reasonably, maddeningly.

"Oh, Jesus, Bert, don't tell me any crackbrained reasons that I'm not thinking of. It's just disrespectful and makes me pee green."

"Willard . . ." The same calm and logical tone; it's a wonder Willard hadn't killed him with a hayfork years before. "You're missing the point entire. This will not only"—he paused and raised one finger—"not only disable the cars of any visitors but will also"—pause, another finger raised, a groan from Willard—"will also put any visitors on our terms, afoot in strange territory, our own backyard, so to speak."

"Jesus, Bert, will you just shut right up. I'm telling you now I want to blow up the road, if you'll just shut right up."

"Get down," Lavenstein said, "and stay down for at least a minute." He wound the detonator up like a noisy, heavy alarm clock, took out the T-handle, and inserted it in the trigger. He handed it to Cookie. "You pop it."

"You mean application is my concern?" She smiled, but he knew she was hurt. Cookie tripped the trigger, the detonator whirred, clicked, the ground bumped, and then the explosion came, deep and louder than you could expect, and then fine rocks, dust rattled in the trees, a few taps as larger pieces rained down and hit other rocks, and the smell of dust and dug dirt.

"See, Willard," Bert said, as if comforting a child getting over a tantrum. "Wasn't that worth it?"

CHAPTER FOURTEEN

She rode to the blast site first, coming up from the ranch side, dismounting. She sniffed at the newly exposed rock, still damp from when it lay in the shoulder of the ridge the day before. She tried to see it as geology, wondering what reached down under her, under the ranch, under the plateau and the range and the coast. Geology was comforting that way; she had enjoyed it at school: the problems of tiny, fleshy people seemed like brief scratchings on the surface of the planet's broad, slow, crystalline life. She would ask someone about the rocks. She picked one up, and its hard weight brought her, reluctantly, back to focus on the problems of tiny people.

The road was impassable. Good. The shoulder of the ridge that had overhung it was shrugged down onto it, over it, and continued down the drop-off into the gorge. It would be difficult to climb over it, loose rock and drying topsoil. If someone came, it would not be by car. It would be along the ridge path above, or through the gorge below and on across the open pastures shoring the Souk.

She remounted Red and unwound Wallace Beery's reins from her saddle horn. Wallace was a large, chocolate-colored quarter horse with a patient nature, not fast, not very bright even for a horse (which put him just above lizards and beetles, she thought), but strong and durable. Wallace was a good soldier. She had him saddled and ready. They backtracked to the ridge-path entrance and started up through the trees to the rocks.

The ridge path turned and turned through the broken ledge at the fold of the ridge, where weather had worn and split and filled the rock. Any friend coming through here would merely swear and complain about Cookie's contrariness. Why go through the damned rock garden when there was a good road? Anyone coming to get Benjy wouldn't get through. It was, she thought, a constricted passage, like Horatius at the Bridge, which Pete had read her as a bedtime story.

"Those behind cried 'Forward!'

"And those before cried 'Back!' " She recited this aloud to Red and Wallace, who were not especially moved by it, no perceptible quickening of the pace or flaring of the nostril. But what can you expect of horses? No culture, she thought. Besides that, she was always a little reluctant to carry on conversation with horses. It exposed a vein of loneliness in her life in the same way the weather had exposed this rock.

On the west side of the ridge, grazing land opened up below her. The blocked road appeared from her left, crossed the creek by a wooden bridge, and turned right, north, toward the highway. Beyond the bridge, in a group of aspens, were the cars, and with them was Francis Fulton Xavier Coyne's car.

She rode up to the aspens and dismounted. She dropped Red's reins—he would stay—but tied Wallace Beery's off on the bumper of Willard's pickup. Both horses began to crop new grass.

"What is this?" Coyne indicated the horses.

"You know, I've been wondering all morning what these bastards are. We made a guess over at the ranch house this morning, and opinion ran high toward 'cow' for a while, though 'doggie' got some votes. What's your feeling, Francis?"

90

"I don't ride."

"Sure you do; you just don't know it yet. And since yesterday, when Lavenstein the destroyer of worlds blew half the ridge onto my road, you either ride or you walk that bulk of yours up and over. I was kidding you. I'm a great kidder, Francis. I do know that these are horses and that they're willing to carry us around to save us from walking everywhere. That's what no one understands. Mysterious, isn't it?"

"You're in a puckish mood, Miss Culler. Humor notwithstanding, I'm here to negotiate a settlement of this thing that will satisfy my clients and your brother and other parties. Riding is not in my line."

"Well, carrying you around is, strictly speaking, not in Wallace's line either, but I have faith that he'll survive the day. You've got to shed a few pounds to join the cavalry, Francis."

"Miss Culler . . ."

"Actually, I'm going to relax just a little, Francis, and let you call me Cookie, because you were defending my honor just a little, weren't you?"

Coyne took a step, no more, toward the horses, viewing them with a sorrowful suspicious look, as if they were machines of destruction. Perceptive man. "How do I get on one of these monsters?"

"Haven't you ever seen a cowboy movie?"

"I will not jump down from the jailhouse roof into the saddle, Miss Culler."

"You could vault over his rump into the saddle."

He turned his head and shot a black Irish look at her.

"Oh," she said. "In that case, we'll go for it conventionally."

She was a good teacher, laying down simple rules to avoid getting kicked and bitten, for steering and stopping, and for rhythm, the essential and not-quite-intuitive skill of riding. Coyne had rhythm, and he was an intelligent pupil, but he had

91

no lines of communication with animals. He stayed up; that was enough for now.

They walked up the long slope to the woods, where the grade steepened, then up at angles to exposed rock. As they entered the maze of trail through the broken rock, she turned in her saddle. He was still on, still looked at Wallace suspiciously. "Relax, Francis. If it helps, his name is Wallace Beery."

"Yes," Coyne said with small annoyance, as a man might respond to comments on the weather when his life was on the line.

They rode on through the fissures in the rocks, sometimes in deep shadow, sometimes in channeled sunshine. "I'm a trusting soul, Francis. I'm taking you to my brother's hideout for this meeting, trusting you more than I should, probably. I don't know why I should bring you through here on a personal tour. This is my bridge, you know. Like Horatius. If anyone tries to get to Benjy through here, my good sword is going to stand a handsbreadth out behind some Tuscan's head. Why should I trust you, Francis?"

"Would a man of ill will ride this . . . this horse?" He said "horse" like one of the nine words banned on radio.

"Besides," he continued, a great effort at sublimating his panic, "it won't be a Tuscan head. It will be a Sicilian head. I made a call. It seems your brother's antics and the investment innovations of the dentists have attracted the attention of the number-one importer. Details are sketchy, but Ben may have used a route and methods and contacts a Sicilian-American group thinks of as its own. They want a piece of the take, and failing that, they want to discourage others. They'll be here. They may have been here already, in the form of that low-grade number in the hospital, the one Lavenstein hit with . . . what?"

"A skillet. His weapon of choice."

92

"Probably just a family relation come out on an easy job to make his bones."

"Bones?"

"His first assignment to kill."

She didn't care to talk for a time after that. Coyne, more relaxed after talking, watched the route carefully, noticing the rocks above them and the corridors between. Then they were out of the ridgeline and descending, rejoining the road. They met Lavenstein walking up the road, carrying the blue pack Benjy had brought, empty now.

"You'll be Coyne," Lavenstein said.

"Good day," Coyne said, leaning down from the saddle and shaking hands, suddenly pretending to be at home on a horse. The saddle creaked as he sat upright again. Some macho thing, Cookie thought, like scratching and pissing higher on trees.

"Where you going, cityboy? You running away?" she asked.

"I'm out of potatoes, onions, want to get some cheese at the co-op, some Beaujolais. Be back toward evening." He turned to go.

"See you then," she called. Lavenstein raised a hand without looking back. He's a cool customer, she thought. If there were any good-looking women around this ranch, I'd think he was having it on. But Lavenstein's famous concentration was part of his famous lack of involvement. He could be attentive, thoughtful, then completely indifferent, as if the nurturing was a thing he did for himself, some expression of needs he couldn't admit. In bed he was like the precise, white-hot point of a cutting torch, roaring and burning. She raised her eyebrows wistfully at the blue pack moving into the woods. Hot stuff, but you can't heat the house with a cutting torch. Did she really want a warm house?

"Cookie?" Coyne inquired.

"See, that's not too silly a name to say, is it? Francis: now that's silly." They rode on.

Coyne had nearly called it all off at the ford. The combination of the horse and the water had been too much for him. He actually made little noises she could hear above the current. But the ride up the mountain had been successful, Coyne suffering less, staying on even when the boys shied and nickered at something in the woods halfway up. She had a camp counselor's pride: Leading the Boston boy down into Wilfred's perfect valley among trees anxious to bloom was a good introduction to horse and saddle.

They had opened into the valley, and they walked Red and Wallace beside the lake, toward the postcard cabin. Cookie turned back to Coyne again, smiling. "Francis?"

"Cookie?"

"Do you have that great big sixty-two-shot automatic on you?" She was, with one finger, unsnapping the strap over her .41.

"Yes. Do I need it? I'm here to negotiate, that's all."

"I hope not, but something's wrong in that cabin. No smoke. Wilfred's an old man. Cold all the time. No smoke. My eyes are going on me, Francis, but I think there's an over-turned cup on the front porch. Do you see that?"

"If you think you see it, you see it. What are you going to do?"

"In about two seconds I'm going to spur up old Red, here, and ride past the cabin on the left side—got that? You get down off Wallace as fast as you can, get out your piece, find some cover, and if any shooting starts, you shoot high, not into the damned cabin. You ready?"

Damn him, there was the slight trace of a smile again. "Whenever you are, Miss Culler."

She nodded once. "Mr. Coyne," she said. A strange man,

but she felt comfortable having him here backing her.

As she turned around she spoke sharply to Red. His ears snapped up, she dug in her heels, and they were off down the trail as if they were after a calf, all of Red's breeding thrown into weaving and running, Cookie leaning low off to the left, keeping Red between her and the cabin, her revolver out, looking under Red's neck like a Cherokee plains raider, passing the corner of the house at a gallop. She rose quickly and in the same movement swung her right leg forward over Red's neck. Her left boot was out of the stirrup and she dropped beside him, running a few steps, fetching up stockstill at the corner of the cabin, her .41 beside her face, pointed up, ready.

No shots. No sounds beyond her own breath and Red scrambling to a cow-pony stop. She looked back. Wallace was standing in the trail with one rein down. Damn you, Wallace, she thought in the midst of everything, don't you run away, you hear me? Coyne was down somewhere; she couldn't see him. Now what, Cookie? she asked herself. The Cookie Culler Swat Team. She took a quick look around the corner. Nothing. No sounds, not even Red now, who was stopped and looked dumbly at her. She stepped around the corner and onto the back stoop. The outhouse door was swung open, a book open on the ground outside it, no one inside. The back door took on a menacing look. Kick it in, dive to the left, and roll. What would Pete have done? Pete was not the diving, rolling type. She knew what he'd do, and she did it. "Hey?" she called, a friendly and confident voice. "Hey, there, this could get sticky, this business with folks outside a house with guns and plenty of time to waste. You want to talk about something?"

No answer. No sounds.

She moved around to the window on the other side of the cabin. She gave herself a quick groundhog bob up and down to look in. Well, there was no gang of desperadoes with bazookas. A longer look. Nothing. Bad feeling. Still quiet enough to hear crows at the far end of the lake.

She turned and started back around the corner to the back door. Her heart plucked, damn, as Coyne came around the far corner at the same time. His clothes were dark with water, his sparse hair streamed down his temples and forehead, the automatic was held in both hands, muzzle up. He'd come through the lake. She gave herself a moment to recuperate and moved in to the door with Coyne.

Charades. She made a window with her finger and looked in. Nothing, she mimed. Coyne nodded, smiling.

He picked up a piece of firewood and pushed up the door latch. The door swung open and stopped against something. Blood showed under the door.

It was Wilfred, a shocking pool of blood around his head, no one else in the cabin. No, Wilfred, Cookie said to him in her most earnest pleading thought. No, you old ranger, don't be dead. Coyne was feeling his neck for a pulse. He nodded, leaned close to Cookie's ear, breathing the words, "Head wound. Blood. Pulse fine. Bleeding stopped." She was watching him, watching his eyes scanning as he breathed quiet syllables to her. "Hit from behind." He pointed with his left hand at a poker on the floor, eyes still moving. "Concussion." Coyne moved carefully through the cabin, wary of the loft, looking under tables, around doors. She wondered if he was looking for bombs and if he had done this in Vietnam. She did not ask but held Wilfred, wiping blood away with a towel. Carefully, Coyne looked out all the windows. Finally he stood. "We've got to get him down to a hospital"—his voice, aloud, was startling—"get some film on his skull. He was hit hard, but he's probably okay. It's the bruising inside the cranium that could check him out." He answered her inquiring look: "My brother the doctor."

96

Coyne went outside, noiselessly. Cookie wrapped blankets around Wilfred and found his ax.

Coyne returned. "No drag marks, no bodies. Where is your brother?"

He was gone. Someone had taken Benjy. But he was not dead. She noted then that she had never been afraid for Benjy, only for Wilfred, as she rode down on the cabin, crept around it. She had known, somehow, that Benjy's life was not at stake. This time.

She took the ax and some braided line outside to cut the saplings she needed for a travois, to drag behind Wallace, to carry Wilfred, to get him off the mountain and into Ellensburg. Where was Benjy?

CHAPTER FIFTEEN

The Souk was strong enough, and Wilfred weak enough, that Cookie worried all the way down the mountain. Coyne walked beside the travois, keeping the blankets tucked as the A-frame racked and twisted on the trail. She could see that he had taken care of wounded before. When they reached the steep mountainside apron of the Souk, Coyne dissolved her fears by stopping Wallace near a stump and mounting with the old man in his arms, gracelessly, unhorsemanlike, but with a deep gentleness remarkable in the large, swaggering man. Cookie saw a moment of it as a single frame from a roll of film: Wilfred's white-haired, weathered, taut-skinned face held close to Coyne's smooth features, his iron-gray hair, his almost feminine frown of concern. This was not a simple man; she could not read him at all. Holding Wilfred, Coyne was not affected by the ford. He continued to hold him long past it, up and into the barnyard.

He gets points, Cookie thought. She would have to trust him even more now.

Coyne found a trailer tire step near the house. Cookie held Wallace's reins as he dismounted with Wilfred, slowly, the old man's blanket-wrapped form making not much of a package in Coyne's arms, even with the boots sticking out.

"I'll get the ambulance to hustle on over from Ellensburg.

They might even have a copter."

"He seems stable. How old is he?"

She added up years, gave him a few less than Pete would have had. "Sixty-six, give or take."

"He looks older."

"Good thing he's not awake to hear you. He and Pete had some hard times together. Didn't get a lot of Club Med vacation time to ease out."

"Pete?"

"My father. They were lawmen together when this was rougher territory, lumberjacks and gold miners and buckaroos on a tear. Some hard cases too."

"Someone mentioned Pete, one of the coffee shop crowd."

"Then why'd you ask?" She was hitching the boys and loosening the girths of their saddles.

"I wanted to hear you tell me about it."

The door was open. Coyne carried Wilfred in and laid him on the couch. They noticed then. Someone had searched the house: cabinet doors were open, contents of closets spilled out, chests thrown open, sheets dumped out of the linen closet.

"Jesus," Cookie said. "When did this happen?"

"After we left, before we came back. Recently," Coyne said, lifting a vase of wildflowers knocked over. The flowers were unwilted, still fresh. He put them back in the vase and filled it, thinking. "Lavenstein left at nine-thirty, we were at the cabin at ten forty-five, it's two-thirty. Someone got our friend here from behind, took your brother, and came down to the house."

"The horses . . ."

"Horses?" They weren't part of his figuring.

"On our way up the mountain, both horses shied at something. I thought it was a coyote or something. Whoever took Benjy was coming down when we were going up." She looked at Wilfred. "Is he okay?"

"For now." Coyne picked up the phone. "How do I get an ambulance?"

"Call the operator and ask for Vern's . . . for the sheriff's line; they'll patch you through, and he'll handle it. Tell him Wilfred's been hurt and to get a chopper if he can. If not, we'll take him over to the Goldweek bridge; Vern'll call us. I'm going out to check the horses—see if they took horses to get out of here."

She stopped for a moment to ruffle Red's forelock, then to pat Wallace's thick neck. Wallace needed the reassurance; stolid as he was, the smell of blood had made him peevish. He'd looked put-upon, carrying the big, evil-smelling strangers. "Poor baby," she said. "Apples later." She slapped Red's neck too, not because he needed it but because he deserved it. Gonna find a man like you someday, Red.

Two horses were gone, two saddles from the tack room, one of them the brown Texas tree that Benjy had favored. Could be Bert and Willard. But it isn't, she thought. Benjy's gone on one of those horses. The horses in the corral were nervous, jolting into one another and having small, meaningless fights, nipping, kicking, but without the desire to connect. She didn't like it. She tried to listen to the horses, listen to the smells, noises, something. Pete didn't help her, and the horses kept milling. She would have let them out to run in the low pasture, but she didn't. She wanted to be near them, though they were flaring their nostrils and rolling their eyes as if an earthquake were coming; she didn't want them to leave her. She was afraid.

She walked around the corral to the north, letting her hand trail on the fence, feeling the texture, listening. From the north side she could look down into the north bottomland, see the Souk skirting the rise of the mountain on the right. Bert was plowing with the Cub tractor that Willard had not ruint

101

after all. She could tell it was Bert by his big, light hat. Then Willard would have been here, would have seen the horses go. She turned quickly.

The hay barn door was not closed, as it should be. I will tell Willard to close the goddamned door when he is finished, she said to herself, very frightened by the open door. Sick, slack in the bowels with plain fear, she willed her feet toward the hay barn, horses moaning and huffling their breath. Coyne was coming down from the house to tell her something about the ambulance, his calling indistinguishable through the corral noises and the rushing of her own blood in her ears.

Her feet stopped her in front of the door. Coyne caught up with her, watching her expression. "Cookie."

"The boys don't like something, and I think it's in there," she said flatly. No, it isn't, there's nothing in there, this is not happening, the horses are stupid and wrong, and we're all okay.

Coyne moved her aside firmly. He had his Browning in his hand and he went in, slipping in from one side to the other in that little patter of feet too small for a fat man.

She walked back to the corral gate, wanting the movement. It was useless to have them here now. She pulled the bar on the gate latch and swung it open. The horses jostled and panicked in their desire to be away. She watched them thunder deftly down the ridge finger that bisected the north and south pastures, rushing north into the new green, up toward Bert plowing far away. He saw the horses coming and waved his hat at her. He was almost finished and would be motoring back soon. Take your time, Bert, she said to him, moving her lips but not speaking the words.

When she turned, Coyne was standing in the open door, a light figure against the dark opening. His automatic was hanging unaimed by his side and he had a sour look of disgust.

She walked toward him. He stopped her at the door. "You

won't want to see this. This is not pretty."

"This is not a pretty business, Francis," she said. "I may need to remember some of the unpretty parts to get through it."

He turned his face away and said, "This is the kind of thing you'll remember too long, after you have any use for it. But maybe you're right. Maybe you've got to see it." He stepped aside.

The light in the hay barn changed as her eyes felt through it. At first, Willard was standing against a post, leaning back and fixing his collar. But he didn't move. Then she could see that his legs were not holding him, and some low intrusion of light through a loose board helped her adjusting eyes see the scuffed, kicked, dug dirt floor around his boots. Willard wore roachstabbers, the pointy-toed, overdecorated boots of a dandy, and she looked at them in the sliver of light with melting spirits. Stained, dampened when he had lost bladder and bowel control, when everything else was shutting down, everything but what must have been a dusty, frantic dance that had kicked motes of hay and seeds and mouse droppings and dirt for yards. Where they were not damp they were dusted, those fancy boots. She sighed as deep as sobbing, and she had to look at his face now, because her eyes were ready, and she wished in the instant that she never had, because she had loved his face in her warmhearted, home-loving way, but this was not the face, not this twisted, terrified, furious, veined, corded expression of fury and disgust. No, she said to herself and to Willard, gently, it's not the face I loved, and I can remember it over cards and over stew and over long-necked bottles. She wanted, more than anything, to untwist the wire, the fence wire, that bit grotesquely into his neck and caught two fingers of his right hand and just the little finger of his left. She moved her head very slowly to the right—she kept a respectful silence, not wanting to disturb any remnant

103

of peace Willard might have left, acknowledging that it was irrational and not caring—to see that the wire had been drawn over Willard's head and pulled tight, catching his fingers, had been twisted once, that then he had been dragged back along the boot marks, kicking and scuffling, from the center of the barn's forward bay to the post, where the wire had been twisted again around the wood, up to the two stick toggles wrapped on the ends. Willard had died there. He had been an angry little man, quick to the insult, loyal to friends. She thought, sadly, that he would not have gone quickly but would have raged away every second left to him. It was on his face. No, she was sure she could remember it other ways: grinning, combing the damned pompadour. She almost reached for the disheveled pompadour, but her hand stopped. There was a stillness here she could not disturb. She backed toward the door and the awful light, suddenly very tired.

Coyne put his arms around her. She could feel where the thicknesses of cloth at his cuffs were still damp from the lake. She shrugged away. "This has gotten bad."

"Sometimes it gets bad," he said, a fact of life.

He went on: "This happened just now, not half an hour ago. Whoever did this, whoever has your brother, is just over that ridge. I can't ride over to see who it is, but you might catch him."

She shook her head yes. Started walking, dazed, across the barnyard, picked up her pace, and was running by the time she hit the front porch. She stopped for a moment at Wilfred, who seemed to be sleeping peacefully, and went out again to Red. She cinched up his girth, mounted, and pulled her Winchester back out of its scabbard. She dropped the lever a quarter throw and saw the brass cartridge in the chamber, closed the lever, replaced the hammer to half-cock, and re-sheathed it. "I'll be back," she said to Coyne. "Take care of that old man."

Red responded to her anger by giving her the best he had: speed, endurance, agility, as they dusted the road behind them and started up the ridge trail. He worked at the slope doggedly and avoided all the obstacles, dancing around them in a heavy grace that would have reminded her of Coyne if she had been less single-minded. Red brought her through the broken rock, threading the maze like a computer wiring diagram, and when they broke into the woods on the other side he let go and came through the trees as if he were running a barrel race. Too late.

There were the two horses, still saddled, grazing free, Sunset and Elspeth. Lavenstein's car was gone from beneath the trees, and so was her pickup. Only Coyne's car remained.

She pulled the binoculars from her saddlebag and scanned the road to the highway. Nothing. Gone. Too late.

Wait.

A car was arriving. Not Vern's, not anyone's she recognized. It was a black Continental, with Illinois plates and two men inside. They passed the horses, passed Coyne's car under the trees, and continued up the road toward the ridge, where they would find the road blocked.

Cookie slung the binoculars around her neck and tucked one tube through her shirt into her bra cleavage so they would not bang about. She turned Red and rode up to the ridge through the trees, dismounted above the slide Lavenstein had made. Both men were out of the car and gesturing at the slide. She focused and watched them, staying low. They wore suits, stylishly cut. The older man's trousers were generously cut, with a full break; the younger man wore pleated trousers tailored slim at the cuffs. The younger man took off his suit jacket and put on a black silk windbreaker with BEARS embroidered on the back. It covered his shoulder holster. The older man unlocked the trunk. He opened two briefcases and assembled two submachine guns, attaching black muzzle

105

tubes that looked like silencers. Cookie continued to watch. The old man gestured, ordering the younger. The old man would go up over the hill, the younger would walk back down through the gully, then come up to the ranch; an admonition to take care, a shaking of the fist—the old man being a disciplinarian, the young man accepting his authority with a curt nod, not enough to be a sycophant but more than the agreement of a full partner. They both set off toward Cookie's bridges.

The warmth, the care and generosity, that made up Cookie Culler had been put aside that day. What had been a fine day with light breezes had suddenly clouded. Storm clouds were rumbling over the pass and the light had turned green; the horses in the lower pasture ran from one place to another. The older man from Illinois cursed, using an old Sicilian phrase, knowing he would be wet. He did not know Cookie, or her ranch, nor did he know about the violence of storms that fall across Snoqualmie Pass when the weather has been worked up.

CHAPTER SIXTEEN

"They're coming," she said to Coyne from her saddle. "Two of them."

The wind had come up, blowing dust and wisps of hay across the yard. Coyne stood at the hitching bar, looking up at the ridge.

"How are they armed?"

"Machine guns, little ones with tubes on the muzzles. Silencers?"

He nodded. "Both across the ridge?"

"One across the ridge, an older guy, the guy in charge. One back down and around into the gully. He'll come out down there." She pointed to the south pasture. Even raised in the wind, her voice had a cold edge Coyne had not heard before. He thought of warning her about vengeance served cold— that was something he knew about—but decided she might need it, if only for the afternoon.

"Did they see you?"

"No," she replied, simply, coldly.

"Is there a pump shotgun in there, and some shot shells heavier than birdshot?"

"Yes. Top drawer, right; buckshot for the coyotes. Can you get up on Wallace again?"

He nodded, one eye squinting against the wind.

"Then you'll have the old guy, coming over the ridge. He's on foot; you have time to get the pump gun and meet him somewhere in the rocks. Does that suit you?"

It made sense. He didn't reply but asked, "You? You'll track the one in the ravine?"

She looked at him, the wind folding her collar up against her neck, a graceful neck and more feminine than she thought it was. The moment she might have spoken passed, and she reined Red around and rode down into the valley of the Souk.

Coyne hitched the reins to a limb with a magnus hitch, something he used on his boat; he was sure it was not designed for horses. He did not walk into the rocks but scrambled up the exposed faces until he was above the maze, looking down into it. He carried the shotgun loaded, shell up, safety on, and a pocketful of shells. He found a vantage that overlooked a straight passage of the rock garden with little cover and waited.

But what if the man coming was wary enough to avoid an obvious trap? One of their people, the kid with the skillet in his face, had not returned. What if he came over the rocks, as Coyne had? Sicily is a rocky country, he reasoned. Getting late for new plans, Francis Fulton, he said to himself. Stay low, move, move. Relieved, he found a cleft with a view of the straight passage below, just deep enough to sink his bulk beneath the surface of the top.

Wind, the damned wind. He listened now, and all he could hear was the wind. Spits of rain freckled the rock around him. He kept listening and looking, trying to use senses no good to him in Boston. . . . Cologne! No, it wasn't balsam or spruce or horseshit; it was patchouli. My God, Francis Fulton, this is a job for a goddamned Labrador retriever and not for a fat mick private dick. He sniffed the air like a bloodhound: There it was again! He watched bits of leaf blow over him for direction. The sonofabitch must be upwind. If this works, I'll write a letter to Fabergé. If this works, I'll get a dog. Don't wait too long, Francis Fulton. He flexed his legs and arms to get circulation, and eased off the safety. Spotty rain coming; now was the time.

He popped up like a cloth clown from a tin box, swiveling left into the wind. The man from Illinois was watching the passage below, crouching but avoiding the rock with the knees of his expensive suit. The movement in the corner of his eye registered, a threat; his reflexes swung him right and brought the MAC 10 right. The man was right-handed, though, and the sharp radius of the turn toward the threat was more than the two-handed machine pistol could accommodate. He shifted farther right with his foot, quickly—he was a man of extraordinary reflexes—but at that moment a high-brass load of number-one shot transferred its energy to his left shoulder, breaking his clavicle in several places, disjointing his left arm, opening one of the descending arteries, and spinning him toward the edge, ruining both knees of the suit. The MAC 10, responding to a reflexive grip by the dying owner, cycled seven rounds with the silencer, no more than a whisper in the wind. Coyne had already pumped up another shot shell and had no way of assessing the damage done. Before the first cartridge clattered down the rocks he fired again, a better-aimed shot this time, and caught the man from Illinois in the center of his turning profile, low on his right rear rib cage. The impact from this last shot, which the man did not hear or even feel, pushed him over the edge. He fell about fifteen feet to the passage below, where he had expected to find someone waiting for him. He had been a wary and intelligent old man, good at his job but out of his element. His body hung on a spur of rock a few feet from the surface of the path. Coyne scrambled down, careful with the shotgun, and re-trieved the machine pistol and a .38 from an old-model shoulder holster. Opening the man's suit coat for the handgun, he smelled again the patchouli. He left the body where it lay, not knowing how quickly crows and little things work.

Cat and mouse. Cookie could play that game with her own variations. She was in her private playhouse, the one she had played in all her life. We'll play, she said to the figure in her glasses, and you can play the cat. At first. She wanted to see his face. It could have been a choirboy's face if the cynicism and disappointment had been scrubbed away by some thorough nun, but it held disregard and boredom out before it like a shield. She wanted to know him; to savor what she was doing, she needed to see him whole. He was chewing gum: Juicy Fruit, Chiclets, Dentyne? His hair was dark and slick, and at one point he paused and passed a comb from his hip pocket through it in a gesture she had seen used by fighter pilots: an unconscious preening, two strokes for good luck. Little shoes, like the first one; he slipped on the cobble collected in the ravine and cursed, in English and in Italian. He held the machine pistol a little too casually, pretending to more of a familiarity than he had. He looked casually, as if he were looking for a pickup on a street corner; he didn't have the systematic eyes of a talented looker. Black silk windbreaker, black pleated pants with narrowed cuffs and a chalkline stripe. White hands, delicate, the hands of a flutist or a floorwalker, holding the black, dull, stamped-metal machine pistol. She watched his face a moment more in the small binoculars, then stuffed one tube down her bra and moved on ahead of him. Another fifty yards, moving easily and quietly, and she broke out into the ravine. She let him see her now.

She remembered a conversation with a cat man from the Barnum & Bailey Circus, vacationing at one of the dude ranches. How you work big cats, he had said, is you let 'em come to get you; you get inside their circle of lunch, get them

110

interested in stalking you, and you move the circle, mean-
while moving them through hoops and across the tubs and up
ladders and shit, because all they care about, all they think
about, is getting to you; then you got to stop them, in such
a way that they can't jump or move on you while you get
inside another cat's circle of lunch; the trick is, of course, not
to get anywhere inside their circle of dinner.

There was a trick to it, and she would feel it out. Risk.
Cookie was not a stranger to risk. Lavenstein came into her
mind suddenly, the thought of Cookie and Lavenstein and
risk. Wrong time; she would think about it later. What was the
range of a little pop gun like that machine pistol? she wondered. Effective range, Pete would say. Okay, she figured,
effective range seventy-five yards, especially if he's not that
familiar with it. She let him see her, then, at between seventy-
five and a hundred yards. She knew he saw her, and she
looked all around, finally calling out, "Benjy, where are you?
Are you down toward the river? What's that? Speak up,
Benjy," and she moved down the ravine toward the Souk.
When she was in cover again she moved quickly, found a
vantage, and watched the boy cross the clearing, saw his look
of satisfied delight, thought she could read the one-up on the
old man in it.

She led him down the ravine, calling ahead to a mythical
Benjy, talking about horses and repairing barns. She thought
of Willard standing in the hay barn and didn't mention barns
again. The rain was starting. When they were almost to the
south pasture, there were distant shots from above, too
blurred by the wind to distinguish them. Cookie had too much
faith in Coyne to worry, and the boy in her glasses obviously
had too much faith in the old man from Illinois.

But were these the people who took Benjy? No, she said,
she'd known that already. That was why she was calling to
Benjy, that was why it was working. These were killers come

111

to kill him, not knowing he was gone. Were these the people who killed Willard? She didn't know that. This boy, though, had come for the wrong reason, and this boy would make the payment on Willard for today. Tomorrow it might be the person who did it. Today this baby-faced street rat.

She opened herself to him, disappeared, moved ahead. She brought him in the rain along a stand of trees, right to the Souk. This was the tricky part. She moved quickly ahead before he could catch up, and when he reached the edge of the pasture cottonwoods she was crossing the rain-dulled Souk on the footbridge above a pipeline crossover. Her neck tingled; she was totally exposed. If he was going to take her it would be now. She banked on the distance, a scant seventy-five yards, a shot made perhaps more difficult by the rain, and on his interest in Benjy. She began to bitch at Benjy: "Benjy, you little sonofabitch, slow down, you hear me? You slow the billy hell down; I'm getting tired." She held her Winchester low in one hand, unthreatening. Keep coming, you bastard.

She went out fast now, up the Minetailing Trail. She doubled back to some rocks and, cautious of rattlers, she worked her way into them. Shading her binoculars against the drops, she watched him cross the footbridge. He was still coming.

He never saw her after that, only heard her ahead of him. He came on up the Minetailing Trail, hearing once or twice a whirring buzz, wondering what it was, then he heard her talking to Benjy, the man they were after, up a side trail. He started up that direction, and his heart almost stopped. A huge snake, the awful kind he had seen in encyclopedias when he was in parochial school, slithered across the trail, larger by feet than he had imagined they could be. Chills, nausea; he wanted to go back and remembered the buzz. God, no; he began to shake. He heard her talking ahead of him. You bitch, you scummy bitch. He waited until the monster had left the trail, then he almost ran up the side trail for her and her scumbag brother, coming onto a shelf in the mountain open to the valley. If there had been sun, it would have been sunny here, and he heard the buzz again from bushes outside the clearing. He wanted to throw up.

The shelf was made by a shift in the mountain that had left an overhanging roof and a flat surface. Rainwater dripped from the picturesque planes of the overhang. But the same shift had fissured the surface below it and collapsed it inward, making a deep pocket with straight sides. Some morbid interest, some evil fascination, drew the boy to the edge of the pit.

Had he lived a long and interesting life, he would never have forgotten what he saw. It was the worst thing he had ever seen. It was a rattlesnake den, where thousands of diamondback rattlesnakes, cold-blooded pit vipers, collect through the winter for mutual warmth or whatever rattlesnakes need. It was a slithering mass of horror for him. He was fixed to the spot on the edge, with a complete loss of motive power, even though several rattlers near him sensed his warm image and buzzed peevishly.

Cookie watched him from above. She drew back the hammer of her Winchester .25/35 and thought about Willard's boots. She fired three shots, each carrying the satisfying concussion and crack of a high-powered rifle, each bursting just behind the boy's legs on the rock ledge, stinging his calves with copper jacketing, startling him in the moment of his worst fears, making him move involuntarily forward, bullying him over the edge and into the awful place. The boy's luck ran out, and he wasn't killed by the fall. She listened to the unbelievably high screams that came out of the den for almost a minute. Perhaps he had been a choirboy, she thought.

She took another trail down to the Souk, crossed by the same footbridge, and walked back to Panama Red. She rubbed his forelock and promised him some apples. He was content with the attention.

Cookie mounted but didn't ride. She sat on Red for five minutes, looking at the stitching around the pommel of the saddle. Pete wouldn't have done that, she admitted. Well, she said to herself at last, maybe I'm not Pete. Maybe times would have changed Pete too. It still didn't sit right. She rode toward the ranch.

CHAPTER SEVENTEEN

Vern had arrived toward the end of the shower. He had ridden one of the horses grazing near the road, Elspeth, up and through the rock garden maze, finding the body of the old, well-dressed man. Vern had come on Coyne beyond the body, sitting near Wallace Beery. "Mr. Coyne," he had greeted him, and Coyne had replied, "Sheriff McKillip."

Vern had asked him politely to put all his weapons down on the grass and move away from them. Coyne thought a moment. "That's a reasonable request from a sheriff who's just come across a body," he said. "Would you object if I didn't put these things down on the wet grass? It just invites trouble later. I can move very deliberately, get up, and hand these things to you."

Vern nodded affably, keeping his right hand unobtrusively near his holster, which seemed to be unsnapped, and he watched Coyne get up without haste or exaggerated slowness but keeping his arms out and his hands around the actions of the shotgun and the machine pistol. He offered them to the sheriff, who sat above him on Elspeth. Vern seemed satisfied with the gesture.

"I'll tell you what, Mr. Coyne. I don't seem to have more than a couple of pockets in this slicker. Why don't you hold on to those for me until we get down to the ranch. I'll wait

115

here for my deputies, so they aren't unduly agitated by our friend in the rocks back there, and then we can ride down. Is Cookie okay?"

"I believe she'll be okay." Coyne's expression told Vern that this was not exactly true. "There's been some bad business this day. Mr. Bottoms has been struck by a poker and may have a serious head injury. Ben Culler has been taken. And two guns from Illinois came to clean up the ranch or get Benjy or eliminate survivors or whatever. Their methods"— he held up the MAC 10—"were drastic. One more thing, Sheriff."

"Yes, sir?"

"A man named Willard, an employee of Ms. Culler, has been murdered. In the barn."

"A friend, Mr. Coyne." Fatigue settled onto Vern's boy face like the shadow of a cloud. He dismounted, tied Elspeth off to a limb, and walked back toward the rock passage, more to be alone than to inspect the effects of number-one shot on old men. He stopped and spoke but didn't turn around. "And Cookie's okay?"

"The other gun went down the ravine over there." Coyne pointed. "About five minutes ago I heard three shots—high-velocity rifle, no automatic fire, no handgun. Would it be your experience of Ms. Culler that she would need more than three shots?"

Vern shook his head. "No," he said. "Do you know why I became sheriff of this district, Mr. Coyne?"

"No, sir."

"Me neither." Vern continued back to the passage.

The Bellew brothers arrived shortly, first one, then the other. They had used Sunset to ride-and-tie and seemed delighted by the body. They were twins, from a ranch at the edge of the plateau, and they loved being deputies, wearing the gray-and-black uniforms, the hats, the badges and guns,

116

and riding around endlessly in a car with big lights. They talked to each other in rapid, unintelligible phrases, a short-hand understood instinctively. They shared a sense of fun and humor impenetrable to outsiders, to whom—that is, to any-one not their twin brother—they never spoke more than a few words. Their chatter over the body, like twa corbies, was unnerving.

Vern told them to pack it over to the ranch.

"Will we get a dust-off for Mr. Bottoms?" Coyne asked.

"We will"—he looked at his watch—"in fifteen to twenty minutes from now. You've used a phrase I haven't heard since the unpleasantness with Uncle Ho."

"You too?" Coyne said simply, not really asking but putting an end to the discussion.

"Me too."

So as Cookie came into the yard from the low side, Vern and Coyne met her. Her face was hard, closed. Vern managed a smile; she did not. Coyne said, "The other gun?"

"Dead." She was unsaddling Red. "Get those saddles off your mounts. These guys have been trussed up too damned long. Have to rub them down, give them a little TLC."

"How?" Vern asked softly.

"Fell. Come on, Vern, shuck that saddle. Come on, Coyne, even you can figure out a buckle and a cinch knot."

"You didn't shoot him?"

"Nope. He fell."

"Well, I'll have the Bellew boys ride over and get him. Where'd he fall?"

"Tell them . . ." She hoisted the saddle off and started into the barn but stopped abruptly, knowing they hadn't seen to Willard yet, and she lofted the saddle up to straddle the top rung of the corral fence. "Tell them to wear some tin pants. Dumb sonofabitch fell into the rattler den up off the Minetailing Trail."

117

Vern's face dropped the pretense of pleasant conversation. His lips drew tight and his chin lifted up to one side, his eyes still on her.

Coyne said, "I'm not sure I understand."

"God damn it!" she said hotly. "These horses have been carrying your asses around for hours; now the least you can do is take care of them. Get away—just let me do this, for Christ's sake. Go take care of Willard if you want something to do, and let me take care of these guys. Dammit, Vern, leave me alone!" Vern stepped back, and his arms, extended, fell.

Vern looked at Coyne as carefully as he could in the dim light, then they untwisted the wire. "Prints?" Vern suggested to Coyne, one crimestopper to another. "Nah," Coyne replied. They found a blue plastic tarp and laid him in it. He was beginning to stiffen; the wrapping was not a neat shroud.

Vern held the wire and toggles. "This familiar stuff to you?"

"Maybe. Could be mafioso, also 'Nam veteran stuff. Whoever it was had time to find two sticks, wrap the wire, and wait."

"Big leap," Vern said, kneeling on the floor of the barn.

"Hm?" Coyne was distracted by the bite of the wire still in the post. He was reflecting that it would be there a long time, a reminder.

"Leap. See? Willard started struggling out here in the middle of the floor, got dragged back to the post." The heel marks were still in the dust.

"He died hard and angry," Coyne said.

They carried Willard out to the edge of the corral and laid him on the ground. The Bellew boys were bringing down the old man, lashed over the saddle. They put him beside Willard, without a tarp.

118

"Boys, I got a job for you." They both nodded at once. "You know the Minetailing Trail here?"

"We can find it, Sheriff."

"Well, a couple hundred yards up from the bottom of the trail is a steeper trail up the fall line. There's a rattler den under an overhang, and this fella's compadre fell into it and killed himself. He's up there now, swole up and hard to get at. Can you boys find a way to drag him out of there? I'm not looking for niceties here. I don't care about mussing him up a little; he's not going to mind. I just don't want you two birds to get punctured too much. Got that?"

They didn't reply but began to converse excitedly in their shorthand language. They passed Cookie, lifting the last saddle off Elspeth. "Machine barn's that way." She pointed with her chin, and the Bellew brothers walked toward it, describing loops, lifts, hooks, and what looked like harpoons with their busy hands.

She took all the saddles into the barn now, avoiding the sight of the blue tarp. She curried the horses and wiped them down, gave them grain in their stalls, and began, with intricate fury, to lather the saddles with the clear, glycerin-amber saddle soap. The smell of it was soothing, all the hours of mindless soaping she had done. She heard the tractor arrive but could not bring herself to go out. She made more rapid circles with the damp cloth on Benjy's saddle. She had worked around to the skirt under the cantle when she heard Bert come in behind her. She stopped but didn't turn around. Don't say anything, don't say a word, Bert. He didn't, but she knew it was him. She dropped the damp pad of rag into the black rubber bucket and it splashed with a hollow gulp. She took the flannel rag from over her shoulder and began to polish the dull residue into a sheen, but she stopped this too. A deep, uneven breath, then she half hitched the flannel around the saddle's pommel and turned abruptly.

Cookie did not look at Bert's face. She knew what she would have seen: an old man's face too near breaking for the umpty-leventh time in a life of hard news and undistinguished disappointment; an old man whose great accomplishments were straightforward skill with large, vegetarian beasts and a capacity for friendship; a man past his prime who had lost the best of friends to one inexplicable mishap after another; a man who held on, who would hold on. She did not look at him because his strength would have made her cry. Cookie did not want to cry now.

She took Bert by the forearm as she strode by him and they walked up past the blue tarp and the body of the Illinois man to the ranch house. Vern and Coyne followed, and when they arrived she was pouring second shots of Jack Daniel's in the mess of the rummaged house. Vern joined them. Coyne put water on for coffee. They all stood at the kitchen counter, staring at the pepper grinder or the toaster or out the window at a section of fence.

The teapot whistled. Coyne rummaged until he found instant coffee. Cookie did not move to help him. Bert handed him the sugar pot. Vern began to move around the house. He checked Wilfred, who was sleeping peacefully, which worried him, and looked at his watch, wanting the helicopter to arrive soon. Coyne came up beside him and said, softly, "This is a search, but not a thorough search. Look—the books are in order, the drawers haven't been dumped. Why not?"

"Dunno," Vern said, flattening a sip of whiskey across his tongue, trying to loosen up enough to think easily. Something was escaping him. "It's wrong. Nothing fits. Benjy's gone, but these two torpedoes come after him. Someone searches the house but does a piss poor job at it. Someone kills Willard, who's got nothing to do with it."

"As far as we know," Coyne said.

"Shit fire, Coyne, that old horse out there was your first-rate mechanic and your first-rate horse tender, but hell, the world outside Cle Elum, or maybe Mamie's over to Ellensburg, didn't mean beans to him. He wasn't a player. And he's dead."

"Too dead."

"Too many goddamned loose ends. Who do these people belong to? The boy Lavenstein got . . ." He began to count on his fingers. "The one who hit Wilfred—and why didn't he kill him?—snatched Benjy, and killed Willard . . . I'm assuming that's one person, or two at the most. These two torpedoes . . . You, Coyne, who owns you?"

"I'm only a negotiator."

"Who carries a gun."

"I'm just as pleased I do, today. And so are you, Mr. McKillip."

"I guess I am. But what about the people who hired you? Do all these other folks belong to them?"

"I don't think so."

"Why, for Christ's sake? Explain just one damn thing to me today." Vern took another sip of whiskey.

"Because they're chintzy bastards on a tight budget. They nearly balked at my price. I'm worth it," he said to Vern's inquiring eyebrows. "But they wouldn't sink the money into all this hardware and muscle. You're right. We're missing something."

The concussive beat of a wide-bladed Huey started suddenly as the National Guard medic copter came over the ridge. Vern nodded. Cookie moved to the couch and tucked Wilfred tighter in his blankets. Vern and Coyne carried the old man out into the barnyard together, and Cookie watched them from the window as the descending helicopter whipped the clearing with its downwash. Straws and chips and pebbles and unidentifiable bits flew and swirled as they loaded the

121

living and the dead. She looked back to Bert. He was not watching but examining with profound interest the very bottom of the tiny glass of whiskey.

Benjy, she thought. Sometimes I'm glad I don't know where you are. But where are you?

CHAPTER EIGHTEEN

She had gone through Willard's things, the detritus of a life spent working at other people's machines, stock, fences. Not much. The usual stack of *Penthouse* and *Playboy,* some prescription bottles for sinus, small, indefinable machine parts, whetstones and three or four worn-thin stockman's knives, hair tonic for the damned pompadour, a thick stack of postcards from all over, done up in rubber bands. She unsnapped the bands and went through them. Some of them were from her, years before when she was in school or traveling. They looked as if they had been thumbed through often, and she wondered when Willard had needed them, needed to think about leaving for far places. We never know anyone, she thought.

She laid out his Mamie's gear, his brown suit with the cream piping around the lapels and the darts over the front pockets. She picked a white shirt, plain broadcloth, and started to lay out a brown-and-yellow tie. But she walked up to the ranch house and returned with something of her own, a string tie with Navajo silver and turquoise. There were three hats. One, picked up from the barn floor, a black Resistol felt, a high roller with a bull-rider's pull steamed in, his winter hat. There was a new straw hat, bought at last year's end-of-summer sale for this summer. Then there was his silver-belly, snakeskin-banded Hoot Gibson go-to-town hat, in a high hatbox with a brush. She remembered that Charlie's boy's cast wouldn't come off for three weeks, and that Willard had always spoken to the boy when they stopped for gas or parts. She took all three hats. His town boots were his special pride. She remembered when he had gotten them. Tony Lamas, lizard skin, with toe clips carved with his initials. They were worth more than his pickup. Willard.

Folding the clothes to take them into town, she saw drops darken the tissue paper and knew she was finally letting herself cry for him. He was like the Souk River or the mountain across the way; he was always there. Her emotion for him would come out slowly.

She left Red in the pasture near the trees and drove into town without seeing the country or feeling the road. Once, when a car came up behind her, she felt for the .41 in the bag beside her, but the car passed and went on. They needed a case of Jack Daniel's and three cases of Olympia, that's what they needed.

She stopped at Charlie's without the usual shouting and went up to his boy's room. She gave him the black Resistol and the summer straw and showed him the silver-belly Hoot Gibson. "I'll take the silver-belly for a few days. It was Willard's outfit for . . ." she was about to say his outfit for Mamie's, but she coughed over it and said, "for town, Saturday night, dress-up. It'll be there at the funeral for show, and then I'll bring it on back to you. You know, we'd pull out of here in the pickup and old Willard would say, 'Charlie's got a good boy there, plenty of sense. Be a good hand when he gets a few years on him.' High praise from a hardworking man. Well, he'd want you to have the hats, and when you get this cast off and this contraption from around the bed, you put one of those hats on and come on up to the ranch. I'll be shorthanded and need someone to get dirty doing smelly work."

He was a serious boy of fourteen, thin with the knobby joints of one who will suddenly shoot up huge, but his face was still a little boy's face, and he turned the hat in his hand as if it were a solid geometry lesson. His serious face concentrated on it, and he nodded. "It's a good hat. A little flashy but a real good hat. If you say he'd want me to have it, I want it. He was a good hand; everybody knew it." He looked at her. "And I don't mind if it's with the body or anything. I don't mind that sort of thing. I just mind Willard being dead. Him and me were going to pan some gold on the Souk this summer. He said so one day while he was getting gaskets for your Cub."

"Bert used to do that. He'd show you how it's done."

"Think he would?"

"Willard's best friend? If Willard made a commitment like that, a serious one to pan the Souk, sure he would. Talk your leg off, though."

"Not this one." The boy pointed at the leg in plaster and traction. His serious face opened an edge, enough for a smile.

She drove to the R.C. church. Gogarty was in the back again, seeing how much of his garden had washed out from the rain. The knees of his dull black trousers were muddy. He was kneeling on a slab of pine and looked up over his shoulder. "Cookie, darlin'," he said, the Boston in it. "You're having a season, aren't you?"

He got up and left the garden. He put his arm around her and took her inside, into his study. "Sit you," he said, a gentle order, while he opened a drawer in his desk and took out a bottle of Black Bush and two dram glasses.

"None for me," Cookie said, unconvincingly.

"Bah. Spiritual comfort needs lubrication. And it's my heritage: trouble and whiskey, whiskey and trouble. Often one's the other with my people, but often not. Often my folks need the Irish can opener to get out what's eating at the pipes inside them. You, Cookie, you need opening, but I don't think

125

even Black Bush will do it. I'd need some walking on water and an acetylene torch along with it to open you up, darlin'. Have another. See? I'll join you."

"Willard . . ."

"I heard, of course. What can I do?"

"I don't know how this works. I mean, I think Willard's people were Baptists or something, but if it's possible, you being his friend and all and you owing him money from the last card game—don't forget that—I was hoping that you could . . . say something, talk a little at the grave, that sort of thing. Is that kosher?"

Gogarty just nodded; he would.

"Simple stuff. We'll go to the graveyard and then over to Vern's and Darlene's for some lunch. Lavenstein's lunch."

"I'd have balked at Lavenstein for the altar boy, but everything else . . ." He nodded again.

She bustled as if to leave.

"Wait," Gogarty said. "Talk a minute more. Talk to me. I'm worried about you, darlin'."

"Me? Hell, Gogarty, I can take care of myself. Worry about Benjy and about Wilfred and about anyone who gets in the way."

Gogarty's face was patient, indulgent. But he repeated the question in the same tone, as if what she had said meant nothing. "I'm worried about you, darlin'."

"Look, Gogarty, I can run the ranch and I can keep off the fucking Mafia and—"

He poured himself another dram, and his voice changed. "Cookie, shut up. Shut up and listen for a change. I'm a priest in a small town, but I do know a thing or two about people. That's why I'm a priest, you know; God's a corporation, and you're one of the stockholders. Damn, I sound like Jimmy Swaggart. But you, darlin', you're a bad poker player and not exactly a daughter of the Church, but in here"—he put the

126

dram down and held both sides of her head like a faith healer—"in here you are the warmest and most generous and strongest woman. And yet you've got a sadness of the spirit, deep, deep inside."

She started to speak and said nothing.

"You're forty-two years old—I've got the records here, you know—and you've never been married; you've slept with half the good-looking men in Washington state, and you're still alone, close to no one."

"Lavenstein."

"Dammit, Cookie, what did I tell you? Do I look like Barry Fitzgerald to you? Am I the local kindly priest? Shit, what you've got with Lavenstein is an arrangement between strangers. I watch you two together.

"Right now all hell is breaking loose. Benjy, who has brought trouble to you any number of times—"

"He's my brother."

"Yes, your brother and your burden and almost your child. He's brought trouble to the ranch, Willard's killed, Wilfred's injured, the boy from Philadelphia—now there's a good son of the Church; I was over at the hospital with him giving him absolution and wanting to hit him with another pot—is hurt, and two more men are dead."

"They came to get us."

"Yes, but if they hadn't followed the trouble here they wouldn't be dead, don't you see? These are lives. But that"— Gogarty banged his fist on the desk—"is not even what I'm talking about. It's you. Holding everything up alone. Big, tough Cookie Culler. Alone."

"I'm fine, Gogarty."

"You're strong. You'll hold on. We both know that. But this is an opportunity, sent from God . . ." He raised his dram glass, drained it, and said, "A word from our sponsor . . . to

127

find the Cookie in you, the one you left behind many years ago, the softer Cookie."

"I'm me, Gogarty; it's all I can be."

"True. Here's a little confession of my own. I know more about you than you know. Father Bartholomew, him that was priest before me, knew about his heart. He kept notes, more than just dates of baptism and such. He was a thwarted psychoanalyst, and he kept notes for his successor. Really extraordinary for a simple man in a small community. There's a section on you, darlin', and some trouble you had twenty-odd years ago. It's buried, and I'm not sure it rests in peace. I want you to know that I know. That I can talk about it without preaching over it."

"I've got to go."

"Finish your drink. Can you do that? Can you talk about it?"

"I don't know, Gogarty."

"You do know that I'm not blackmailing you into saving your soul, don't you? And you must know that I want only good for you, as your friend. Can you think about it, and we'll talk?"

"I'll think about it."

Gogarty held up his hands, surrendering to fate. "All I can ask. One more thing. The family called from Boston about Coyne."

"What about him?"

"Strange man, it seems. Was a lawyer, respected, partner in a criminal law firm. Frustrated by the process, by the police. Details are sketchy, but he pushed the limits more and more. Even roughed up some defendants who'd threatened his clients. Was up for disbarment once or twice, but it never stuck. Very bright, very intense. Drank. The Curse." Gogarty toasted the Curse as he nipped off another dram. "As troubles accumulated around his professional and personal head, he drank more. His wife divorced him, took his two children and

128

moved away, no one knows where. Changed her name. Gone. Coyne, it seems, became a private negotiator, an investigator who specialized in persuasion. Not exactly a heavy but willing to lean if it helps. Not a killer, not a hired gun. A forceful negotiator with a reputation for being dangerous to meddle with. End of report. The Gogarty boys and girls of the force were of mixed feelings having him out of Boston. On the one hand he was a magnet for trouble. On the other hand he was known to work out deals between sides that usually worked things out in broad, loud mime. Bang, bang." Gogarty pistol-pointed his finger. "Strange man."

"Good man in a jam," she said. She was still thinking. She was hurt, angry, unwilling to disinter old wounds in the midst of new hurts.

"I know, I know," Gogarty said. "Forget about it all for a while. But force yourself a little later and talk when it comes easy. Come talk to me."

She got up. Gogarty rose unsteadily. She put her arms around him, and he hugged her warmly.

She held on. She could feel the warmth of the man, smell his Black Bush and black wool and his male, pleasantly doggy smell. She felt loved. It was not a feeling she often allowed herself. She broke away. "Saturday," she said. "I'll call with the details."

"I'll talk with the funeral home and with Darlene," he said.

She left, and Gogarty went through the kitchen to resume his gardening but decided he was more needful of a nap.

She rang the back-door night bell, though it was the middle of a cloudy, chilly afternoon. Jim Stottlemeyer answered the door, a heavy one with three locks, wiping his hands with a towel.

"Three locks, Jim? People are dying to get in here?"

"Mostly for show, I think. And for curious, weird drunks,

want to come and see the grisly stuff. Plus, folks are fussy about their dear departed being seen or joked about with in what you might call a vulnerable state. Want to come in?"

"No, I'll just stay out here."

"Come on in, Cookie. We'll sit in the office, right in here. Nothing weird about that. Hey, I deal with this all the time, and I understand that you don't. Old days, people did the best they could for grampa or gramma right there in the parlor: got what ice they could, threw the strongest cologne and flowers they could get around to mask the . . . ah . . ."

"Decay," Cookie said.

"Yup, the decay. All this stuff"—he waved his hands around him—"wasn't popularly available until the Civil War." He sensed that his little lecture on mortuary science was wearing on her and changed the subject abruptly. "You bring some clothes for Willard?"

"Hey, Stottlemeyer, he's not going to look bad or anything, is he? I mean, his expression won't . . ."

"No, Cookie, don't worry. I got that taken care of, and the laceration around here"—he put two fingers to his throat—"all okay. Looks good."

"The pompadour. It's got to look real fine."

"Not to worry. Hair spray. Looks great."

She laid out the clothes on the desk. "Good suit," he said. "A lot of seams. Jesus, Cooks, I don't know about these boots. You know yourself how difficult it is to get on a good pair of boots when you've got your foot helping. Oh, I could get them on him, but you see"—he ran his finger up the back—"I'd have to cut them all the way up. Damn shame, boots like that. Now, we've got boots, funerary footwear, that look good from the front, look like simple boots, a little stitching." He traced some imaginary stitching on the toe of the Lama boot.

She nodded. "How about this, Jim? How about we put the

boots and the hat, here, off to one side on a table or something, kind of a Willard-the-dude table."

"Yeah, we could do that real nice. Anything else on there?"

"Maybe a little candy dish full of prophies, to show what the outfit was for." They both broke up, partly out of guilt and partly out of relief.

CHAPTER NINETEEN

"It's the new look, Wilfred," she said as she came into his room. "Punk old man."

They had shaved the left side of his head to expose the break in the scalp. The stitches in his inelastic old man's skin puckered around black suture ends, prickly and straight like the thin thorns on cactus leaves.

"You just rein back on that 'old man' horseshit, little girl. If it was you hit with a great iron bar from behind, you'd been dead three times over. Add to that being dragged by my heels down the goddamned mountain and left on the living room floor to bleed, while you and the mick have target practice with some poor confused guineas from Chicago."

"That mick carried you half the way, old man, as if you'd been worth it."

"Carried me like a sack of Irish potatoes, feels like. Sore all over from rough handling when I couldn't protect myself against it. It's a wonder someone didn't take advantage of me."

"How do you know one of these little candy stripers didn't?"

"You know, now you mention it, there is one always comes in looking smug and asking if there's anything special she can do for me. I'll bet you're right. I'll be damned if that little butter-wouldn't-melt do-gooder wasn't—"

"Wilfred, I'm worried more about your blood pressure than about her lapse of medical ethics. Settle down and live longer. Tell me something—how'd they get you?"

"With a big iron bar."

"With a poker. How did they get down in the valley without your knowing about it?"

"I don't know, dammit. I didn't hear anything out of the ordinary: ducks mating, owls; nothing unusual at all. I came out of the outhouse at six-thirty, just like I always do, clock-work, like I told you, and blam. I'm down."

"I can't remember—which way does the outhouse door open?"

"Out."

"I know that, for Christ's sake. Does it hinge on the left or right?"

"Looking out or looking in? I told all of this to the mick."

"Then tell me again, you crotchety old feeble-brained tur-key!"

"It hinges on the right looking out of the outhouse. And the mick plays a bad hand of gin."

"He's been here?"

"Every day since I've been awake."

"Yesterday and today, Wilfred."

"More than I can say for you."

"I'm here today."

"Yes, you may say that, but you weren't here early."

"You're an impossible old man."

"My prerogative. As an old man and as the probable parent, in this case."

She'd had enough of death and sickness. She had sat with Wilfred all afternoon, made up for Coyne's lack of skill at gin by putting the old man fifteen dollars in the hole, and had sat

134

beside him as he slept, on and off, his head, shaved and discolored and stitched together, more painful than the old man let on.

Wilfred's surgeon had shown her the CT scan. There was no bruising inside the skull that could cause dangerous pressure. They would keep him in the hospital for a week to watch him. Did he have medical insurance? Did he have veteran's benefits? Did he have Medicare?

She offered to take him to the ranch and watch him there. The doctor shrugged. "He's got to have some benefits. Cowboy benefits, probably."

"What's that?"

"That means that his pickup's not worth repossessing and his wages aren't worth attaching."

"He's got them, all right. Except there's no pickup."

The surgeon smiled. "Well, we won't throw him out back. Maybe we'll get him out a little early, though."

She had gone to Mr. McGregor's for the happy hour, and she took advantage of it. She couldn't find any songs on the jukebox that were sad enough. "So this woman runs away with this other guy and it's planting time and three little kids to feed," she'd said to Tom behind the bar, "and he's broke up. Big fucking deal. Kids'll be fine. Get planting done. Find woman with better tits, my advice."

Now, at the motel, she banged on the door for half a minute before Coyne opened it. "Hey," she said to him, "don't worry. I brought my own." She held up a square bottle of Mr. Daniel's best.

"Come in out of the cold," he said. He was wearing a thick sweater and corduroys and sheepskin slippers with soles. She came in and went straight to the bathroom for a glass. Coyne's things were laid out neatly on a towel. When she came back in, he had poured two cups of coffee from a travel pot on the dresser. "How about a cup of good coffee?" he

135

asked. "I have this ground at Cardullo's on Harvard Square. It's a mocha coffee."

She took it and tasted it as she sat down on the bed. "Good," she said, and poured a finger of Jack Daniel's into it. "Mm. This is good too."

Coyne wrinkled his eyes: whiskey in good coffee.

"Cool it, Boston. Cool it." She took another sip. "It's really good, I told you that, and I don't want any lectures, any preaching, any death or destruction, don't want to hear a discouraging word. Seldom."

"What are you doing?"

He was working on the round table near the door. It was covered with papers, yellow legal pads, a CD player with earphones, and a box of macaroons. He picked up a pad with two circles on it and names inside them. "Two groups after Benjy. One group is the Charleston group, and I think the controlling factor there is money. Also, I think I am their only agent, unless they have funds beyond those I suspect.

"Second group. The Mafia. Controlling factor here is power: who licenses the illegal flow of narcotics, who establishes safe routes, which shouldn't be compromised by amateurs."

He drew another circle on the pad. "But look: I'm in place, Group One, ready to negotiate, and Benjy is taken. Just after he's taken, Group Two shows up to prove how nasty it is to fool with Mamma Mia, not knowing he's gone. Group Three. There is a third faction here.

"Now I step back. Think of this a different way, I say."

"This bores me. This different way bores me."

"Stick with me. Think of this thermodynamically, I say."

"The first way bored me too."

"Input/output. Simple equation. How much dope can you pack into the cockpit of a Long-EZ? Enough for three factions? Enough to account for me, three hoods, and a separate

136

faction? No; something's wrong. Something doesn't compute."

Cookie sat up from her slouch back on her elbows. She put her coffee and whiskey on the bedside table. "How much can you pack in? Now, Francis, you've touched on an area of my expertise." He was Cute.

She undid her cuffs, watching them closely, and then she watched Coyne, smiling a Cookie smile as she undid the buttons of her shirt, a blue oxford-cloth button-down. He was uncomfortable. Good. Damn, he was Cute.

"Hold up, there," he said.

"Right," she replied, and pulled the shirt off one arm, then the other. She was wearing a white cotton polo shirt under the blue, and she stood up for this. She undid one button and pulled it over her head, shaking her hair free and loose as it came off. She cupped both breasts in her hands. "Packing it in, exhibits A and B, Francis. Now, about exhibit C, a necessary part of our case . . ." She took a step toward him.

"Cookie." His voice was soft, full of regret. "I can't do this."

"What's the matter, Francis?"

"You are very beautiful. You are . . ." He turned his head away. "This is too hard, really. May I ask you to put your shirt on?"

She felt chill, suddenly, and angry. "What? You really are a homosexual? You don't go for ladies, Francis?"

He made a deep, pained noise, like a bull elephant having a bad dream. "No. Here." He got up out of his chair and held the oxford-cloth shirt for her, delicately, as if he knew how women dressed in the morning.

She buttoned most of the buttons and turned to hit him. At least that is what she began to do, but she let her fist come down and she put her forehead against his convex chest, against the thick sweater and the smell of soap. "You don't

137

like me. I'm too brassy and dykey for you."

Coyne put one arm all the way around her. With his left hand he lifted up her chin, and he kissed her warmly, deeply, a kiss that balanced unsteadily between what she wanted and what he was trying to preserve. He broke away, not quickly but more quickly than she wanted. He picked her up, quite easily, and held her against him as he sat down in the chair. She felt warm and good. "I don't turn you on," she said.

He snorted. "Quite the contrary," he said. "I think you are a shining woman. You've been grating against my composure since I saw you the first time."

"Then . . . ?"

"I'm in love, Cookie."

"With your wife, the one who took the kids and left you?"

A raised Boston eyebrow: You've been doing your homework too. "No. I botched that relationship beyond any hope of repair. I have no right to intrude on that good woman any further. This is a woman in Newton, outside Boston. A researcher with two kids of her own, young kids. She's a few years younger than I. Cookie, I'm very lucky, to be able to love again. I have promised myself that I will do better with this one than the last."

"I'm sorry."

"You're so attractive to me that I must be very careful. If it weren't for that, I'd . . . who knows?"

"You're too fat anyway, Francis. You've got to lose some pounds." She nestled into him. Hold me, Francis, don't let me float away.

"I'm forty-two. My hips are too big. My tits are getting flat. I've got these little wrinkles around my eyes." She was crying, but Coyne was kissing the little wrinkles, and that made it better.

"Why are you with Lavenstein?"

"He loves me. Well, he likes me a lot. He knows me."

138

"Then why are you here with me?"

"We have an arrangement. No strings, no obligations, no jealousies."

"Arrangement. That's like a coffee table arrangement. Artbooks here, *New Yorkers* here . . . formal, cold. How much does he care?"

"He cares if I'm upset."

"When will he leave?"

"Soon." She said it before she knew it, she knew it was true, that his paper would be done and Lavenstein, the city boy, the destroyer of worlds, who lived in an abstract life of long wires, deep concentration, and short commitments, would be gone soon. He might come back, as he had before, to hole up and work on another paper. He might.

"He's good in bed," she said. Hold me, Francis.

"That's about a third of things, even when it's going well. Cookie. Tell me this. You are beautiful and smart and strong and wonderful: Why aren't you married, with six kids?"

She nestled in farther. She took his arms and made him hold her hard. He was a strong man, big. Pete would have liked him. She was crying. An old door opened, the one Gogarty had unlocked, the scary door with the hinges that creaked, and the pain was scary even inside Coyne's big arms.

"What?" he said. "I didn't hear you."

"I did. I had a baby." He knew enough not to say anything. She was shaking; he held her. "I was nineteen. I was screwing around with—"

"Don't say that."

"But I was. I was screwing around with this guy I'm not sure I even liked. My mother fixed it. I went to Portland, went to school, took classes in everything, waited. She fixed the whole thing up. Last thing she did for the family."

"Where is she now?"

"Seattle. Lives in a condo with the lawyer she left Pete for.

139

Flashy sonofabitch. Rich. She took Benjy.

"I had the baby and they took it away from me. It was a little girl. They told me a nice family adopted it. A farm family, they said. She'd have a nice place to grow up in—maybe they tell that to nineteen-year-olds." He held her.

"I dream about her. She's grown up now. I . . ."

"Ghosts, Cookie. The past is full of ghosts."

"Hold me, Francis. . . . I went away when Benjy needed me most. Mama was leaving. Pete needed me. She needed me, tiny little girl, and I let them take her away. But I held her for a little while. I . . ."

He had begun to rock her.

"I sang to her too. Sang her name."

"What was her name?"

"No." She tried to stop crying. "That's all I have left. That's mine. I sang it to her, and she heard it. It's all that's left of us."

"I could help you find her."

Now she did stop crying. "No. I drew the mount and I'll ride it. Pete never knew. He thought I was going away because the marriage was going to hell and Benjy was acting up. Jesus, I let them all down, Pete and Benjy and my mother . . ."

"Do you ever see her?"

"No. She let us all down too, but she was meaner about it."

"About your mother. If I'm any example, Cookie, I can tell you that you do things in your life that you can't explain later."

The boy beside the rattler den imaged and faded in Cookie's mind, as she knew he would the rest of her life. The pitch of his screams, though, would probably come only at night.

"You should have had more babies."

"Well, I'd sent her out into the world without her mother. I'm ashamed of that, Francis. That's what you'd call a sin; it's

140

not adultery or theft or blaspheming or any of the other things we call sins. Sinning isn't easy, Francis. Most people think they've sinned and don't know what they're talking about. They've fucked around or juggled figures or have just been rude. No. Sliding out of a bind at someone's expense, hurting someone helpless, doing something you live with the rest of your life . . . Sin kind of assembles like a kit, and then it's there in the middle of the living room forever.

"So I sent her out there alone, and I've never felt fair about giving better to another. Too late now. I'm too old."

Coyne rocked her, nodded. After a time, he said, "There are some problems that don't have solutions."

She nodded with him and said, "Hold me, Francis."

Coyne was still rocking her, enjoying the warmth of her in his arms, when the phone rang, half an hour later.

He picked it up and answered. "Coyne."

"Mr. Coyne, this is Vern McKillip. Is Cookie there?"

He knew better than to deny anything to a small-town sheriff. "Right here, Sheriff."

"Good; good to know she's in safe hands. Look here, I wonder if you two would like to meet me at Mr. McGregor's in, say, ten minutes? There are a couple of fellas, one of them watching your place and being watched by one of the Bellew boys, that we might find interesting in this case of ours."

"We'll be right down, Sheriff. Should we take any precautions coming out?"

"Oh, I don't think so. The Bellew boy, there, won't let anything untoward happen, but I'd bring along your piece, if I were you."

"What's going on?" she asked, as Coyne stood and set her on her feet.

"McKillip. How did he know you were here?"

She grinned. "Vern looks out for me," she said. "Has since fourth grade."

Coyne shook his head. Small towns. "Splash some water

141

on your face, Cookie. We're going down to inspect a new set of torpedoes at Mr. McGregor's."

She turned away and took off the oxford-cloth shirt to put the polo shirt back on. Coyne watched her smooth-muscled back and shook his head again in a rattled, hopeless way. He laced on his shoes and heard her in the bathroom take a pee, splash water on her face, use his toothbrush, and reappear looking fresh. "Okay, Francis, let's go get 'em."

"You think you'll ever grow up?"

"With luck I may avoid it."

Abruptly Coyne took her in his arms again. He held her and kissed her temples, one side and then the other. "But if you manage to grow up, little girl, you may manage to forgive yourself. You're worth it."

He turned away, and she didn't have a snappy reply, any reply. Just before they left the room, Coyne ran back the slide of his Browning automatic, checked the magazine, and felt for the spare in his pocket.

CHAPTER TWENTY

Mr. McGregor's, midnight. The bubble lights and the neon were doing their best to ignore a night of light, cold rain. Spring comes hard to Cle Elum. Vern was sitting in Cookie's booth, facing the door, drinking coffee and a draft beer.

"Evenin', Cookie. Mr. Coyne, a pleasure as ever." The two men shook hands in a formal but friendly way, two software salesmen staying at the same hotel.

Tom came to the table with a coffee for Cookie, tactfully avoiding her eyes, since she had played the same song five times before she left earlier in the evening. He brought a club soda for Coyne; he'd put a little Japanese umbrella in it. Coyne picked out the umbrella with his thumb and forefinger, delicately. "Thank you, Thomas," he said acidly. Tom allowed himself a thin crescent moon of a smile as he wiped the table.

"Tom," Vern said, looking across the room at a neon Olympia sign, "you might get a case of the shakes in a while. Might drop some loud, disruptive article over behind the bar while Mr. Coyne and I are going to drain the monster. You feel shaky, Tom?"

Tom reached to wipe the far side and knocked over both salt and pepper shakers. Picked them up, left with his tray. "I thought we had the corner on those silent types in Vermont," Coyne said.

"Don't know where Tom's from," Vern replied amiably. "He never said."

"So. Where are the new torpedoes? More Chicago?"

"I don't think so, Mr. Coyne. Mr. Princeton is sitting over by the door, pretending to drink Scotch. Mr. Yale just walked in. Sitting down with him. He was the one watching your place."

"I'd file an invasion-of-privacy suit, but the community doesn't run very deep in privacy."

"Of a kind, Mr. Coyne, of a kind. Cookie, sashay over to the bar and get us some popcorn, will you?"

She was back in a minute, stopping to talk with P.J. and friends, no hard feelings.

"Cookie," Vern said, "you're a handsome woman. Attract every eye in the place. 'Cept those fellas. What do you say we join them, Mr. Coyne?"

"It's direct and friendly. I like it," he replied.

They rose and started for the men's room, but two bottles of seltzer water Tom was carrying dropped and exploded, bar sitters scraping back their stools, drinks flying, bar rags flourished, and suddenly Coyne and Vern were sitting outside the two young men, each about thirty, pressing them in a friendly but confining way against the paneled wall. Cookie joined them.

"Well, here we are, all together," Vern said. "I know that you fellas have an interest in Ms. Culler and Mr. Coyne, and the sheriff of a small place like this is just an extension of the chamber of commerce, you see. Now, of course, I don't know the nature of your business, so I can't help any further."

They said nothing.

"What do you think, Sheriff McKillip?"

"I don't know, Mr. Coyne."

"Well, my friend over here has a small automatic in his belt. I can feel it. Uh-uh, sport, look under the table here; I've got

144

a big automatic. See? Mine's bigger than yours.

"Do they look like hoodlums to you, Ms. Culler?"

"No, they do not, Mr. Coyne. They look like accountants. I like the way they keep their nails."

"Boys, I am the sheriff, and I'll have to take these pieces first. Then I'll have to ask you for some identification, permits to carry, that sort of thing."

Princeton spoke. "We'll have our attorney speak with you. We are legitimate law officers."

"Well," Vern said, with a reticent sadness, "usually your legitimate law officers, by which I mean the ones who aren't genuine bastards, carry all kinds of identification. Kind of a gesture of good faith."

"We're under deep cover."

"Then pull them up over your heads, boys. You're spending some time as a guest of the town. I fear it's not as comfy as the Ramada Inn. Let's step out into the parking lot, shall we?"

Vern searched the pair, gave Cookie the identification they found: drivers' licenses registered in the District of Columbia, membership in Courts Royal Racquetball, Arlington, Virginia, credit cards, Riggs Bank cards, Hertz cards, AT&T Calling Cards. Vern turned and murmured, "Cookie, you may want to disappear with those for a moment while my back is turned and ask your computer pirate friend, Mr. Bering, what he comes up with. I'll go through channels, but I don't believe I'll find a thing." She walked to the phone inside the door.

Coyne was standing behind the two, his Browning leveled, as they leaned against the wall with their feet spread. "They may be carrying more illegal weapons," he suggested happily. "Let's search their car."

"Can we do that?"

"If Washington law is anything like Massachusetts law, you can. You've already found them carrying concealed weapons

145

while acting in a suspicious manner. We can go through their underwear, if we want."

"Let's start with the car."

Cookie returned and gave the identification to Vern with a nod. "Tomorrow sometime, with luck."

"The car, boys."

They found the rental Thunderbird at the far end of the parking lot, identifying it from the plastic Hertz tab on the key ring. The two men were saying nothing, though their sullenness was burring around the edges into nerves and anxiety. Vern opened the trunk and turned to hand the two small automatics, Walther PPK 9mm's, to Cookie. She stepped between Coyne and the two men to take them. Yale, the one nearest Vern, leaped like a member of a Chinese dance troop into a wide fighting stance and swung his leg toward Vern's head, but he stopped as the tire iron Vern was holding connected with his shin. Vern dropped the iron back into the trunk and hit Yale with his fist, purely out of spite. Yale fell onto the asphalt.

The other started for Cookie and the guns, but Coyne stepped between. Coyne put away his automatic in his jacket pocket, and the little smile flickered around his face like the transparent flame of a gas burner. "Watch this," Cookie said to Vern.

Princeton assumed a stance, bobbed, and made claws of his hands; emitting several feline noises of concentrating power, he bounded up toward Francis Fulton Xavier Coyne. Coyne waited, too long, it seemed. But just as Princeton had committed himself to one thrust and was leaping through the air to deliver it, Coyne vacated that particular air and was well placed to injure the young man as he passed. Princeton fell in a heap, unconscious.

In the trunk they found two foam-lined briefcases with machine pistols.

"What in hell are these?" Vern asked.

Coyne took one of them. "Heckler & Koch MP5 SD one hundreds. Nine millimeter. Silencers." He screwed on the black tube and looked at the assembled piece in the light of the streetlamp. "Not your standard peace officer's kit."

In a flatter, longer case, Vern found a take-down rifle with a telescopic sight. He glanced at the bore. "Good lord, is this for buffalo? This must be fifty caliber."

Coyne took it from him, looked it over, and handed it back. Drop-block single shot, seven-power starlight scope. He reached into the case and took one of the huge rounds, shaking it gently, listening. "I've only heard about these things. This is a sniper's rifle, what the Seals are using for high-priority hits." He held out the cartridge to Vern. "Explosive heads, meant for blowing gas tanks, and the car and the passengers with them, at a thousand yards plus. We're into a very weird area," he said. "This isn't mob stuff; this is government, intelligence, trouble."

"God damn it!" Vern shouted. The Bellew brothers, standing nearby with their pieces drawn, walked into the light.

"What is it, chief?" one of them asked.

"Not a goddamn thing, Bellew. Too many goddamned things. I hate complication, and this is getting out of hand. Let's take these two acrobats downtown."

Cookie and Coyne and the Bellew brothers looked at Vern quizzically. Downtown Cle Elum?

CHAPTER TWENTY-ONE

Panama Red waited patiently, staked out in the grass.

"You big handsome hunk," she said to him. She ran her hands over his smooth coat, almost fox red, feeling the packages of muscles beneath it, admiring the boxy power of quarter-horse breeding. "You're not slim, Red." She scratched between his ears. "You're no ballet dancer, are you? You're a major machine, though—yes, you are."

She saddled him and rode up through the rock garden and down onto the tongue of high ground over the Souk, to the ranch house.

Lavenstein had breakfast ready—venison sausage and fried apples with biscuits, kept warm on the wood stove.

She sat down to the place set for one and began to eat. Nathan sat in the corner, immersed in his paper.

"Good," she said.

He nodded.

She buttered another biscuit. "I spent the night with Coyne."

He nodded. "Oh? Everything's okay in town?" Nathan made some marginal notes on his paper.

She couldn't eat the biscuit. She couldn't watch Nathan going through the stacks of papers. She tried to begin again. "Wilfred's coming along. He'll be out of the hospital in time for Willard's funeral. Saturday. Gogarty's reading the service. Says you can't be altar boy."

"What's the matter, Cooks?"

She looked at the biscuit, looked out the window. "I didn't sleep with him, Nathan."

"Hey, Cookie, it's up to you. We're grownups. We're our own people. We don't watch over each other. There's no guilt here. We're together because we want to be, when we want to be." He went back to his papers. Stacks of papers, like stacks of *National Geographic*s on a coffee table.

She went back to the biscuit for a time. She took it, careful not to drip honey, and walked across to the window that looked down into the south pasture. With one hand she rearranged the pussy willows she was trying to force into bloom.

"How's the paper coming, cityboy?"

"Soon, soon. A few more days and it'll be done."

Maybe it was just too early to force blooms. Maybe the winter had been too hard.

She ate the biscuit anyway and attacked the dishes. Lately she had noticed a slight tendency in herself to stand and moon about. She was not against mooning about in principle; it was simply that her neurons and circuit boards were set for immediate, sustained action: Go For It Cookie. There was a new need, though, a diagnostic program running through those circuit boards, querying those rapid-response neurons, something new or old, something that had been ignored in the blur of motion, and the questions came slowly, interrupting the slamming, clumping comfort of her loud life. Mooning, her mother had called it. She watched the water drip from a cup until cup and drip and the white lace pattern of suds blurred, as she wondered how her mother had become part of this. Her mother, who was with the lawyer in Seattle as surely as damned souls are in hell. And how did hell get in here?

There were not many dishes. Nathan was the kind of cook

who cleaned as he went. She washed and rinsed and stacked, still moving at the slow walk this new confused introspection demanded. It was as if a friend came by when you were trying to get work done and picked up this tool or that one, humming, obviously waiting to say something, avoiding a subject, but you were not quite yet to the point of saying, Out with it, for Christ's sake.

She dried her hands, liking how clean and soft they felt after the washing. I've gone broody, she said to herself, half disgusted, half amazed because what she wanted was to sit down and talk. Not at Mr. McGregor's over long-necks. She wanted to talk with another woman, like Darlene or Millie.

Five minutes later she was scaring the horses. They hated it when she mucked out the barn like this, with a hair across her ass. They milled in the corral and watched the intermittent plume of hay and horseshit fly out the doors of the barn like dirt from a badger's dig. Nathan Lavenstein, destroyer of worlds, could take his paper and shove it. She leaned for a breathing space on the fork and wondered for the first time if Lavenstein was such a bargain. A great lay, she concluded, starting the mucking again, not to be missed, but there may be more out there.

The round table was full. Lavenstein sat, or rather visited the chair, nearest the kitchen counter. Cookie sat across from him. To her right fidgeted Wilson and Charlie Bering, both of them reading the labels on cans and bottles of food, like rat terriers after the vermin of a corrupt society, crowing as they discovered various slow poisons. To her left two larger, calmer hunting dogs, Vern and Coyne, sat quietly with their hands folded around coffee mugs. Vern seemed unimpressed at the terriers' discoveries, but he had been known to eat five Devil Dogs with a single cup of coffee, and after Darlene's cooking (a dear woman, a great cheerleader, but . . .), a little

151

monosodium glutamate made his mouth water. Bert was in Ellensburg, visiting Wilfred for the evening.

A thin person could have subsisted, like some tropical orchids, on the air in the kitchen. It was rich and redolent of slow cooking, of the caramel residue from natural sugars browned in tune with solvent wines, of the bitter thinness in rosemary and the round poetry in bay, of roots warmly revealing their higher nature, of the exotic Indies inside the simply cracked peppercorn, of the slightly sour lubricity of butter in a hot pan.

They drank Olympia, a passable light lager, from pitchers on the table. Lavenstein insisted that beer needed the space to breathe as much as wine, for he was no oenophilic snob about beer. Coyne drank Calistoga water. There was a bowl of kalamata olives, a piece of Tillamook cheddar, and a small ash-covered roll of chevre beside a rick of pita wedges. Coyne made notes on his yellow pads, Wilson cackled over government decisions and blew incompetence into scandal, Charlie Bering corrected his loose-jointed figures and cautioned his loose-moraled speculations, Cookie listened to the two of them, and Vern watched Cookie. Lavenstein prepared to present.

Appetizers and pads were cleared away. Charlie and Vern were pressed into service. Wilson saw himself as the dinner guest who brings the wit, feeling with some fluctuating justification that wit is a major contribution that precludes serving and cleanup. In the delicate social structure of dinner parties, Coyne was the new guest and would not be asked more than, perhaps, some light cleanup. The table was ready.

First, plates of vegetable salad: new asparagus up from California on beds of red leaf lettuce with bitter crisp slices of endive, sweet slivers of red bell pepper, capers, pecans, and a raspberry vinaigrette.

Now the pitchers of Oly were taken with the salad plates,

152

and the meal itself arrived, a peasant meal if peasants were doing very well. There were cool bottles of a good California zinfandel and big burgundy glasses. A towel-turbaned basket wisping out the fragrance of corn bread with cheese and chilies baked in it. A great blue bowl deep with elk meat stew: chunks of haunch, carrots, a hundred pearl onions, peas, sweet parsnip rounds, celery soft beyond recognition, and a red wine sauce to swim in. And, with a flourish, a long platter of twice-baked potatoes, laden with onion bits and grated Romano and chives and cream. Charlie, who was a cheerful vegetarian, literally rubbed his hands at this entrance, and even Wilson's nonstop conversation with himself was masked to unintelligibility by the food. The only other sounds were the rude and guttural praises of hungry eaters eating.

Coffee, Loomis Valley apples, cheese, and chocolates. Coyne had taken over the cleanup, guest or no, and was predictably efficient, turning washed and rinsed dishes into the drainer faster than two people could dry. Lavenstein returned to his corner with his cup, not to resume work but to gloat at the effects of his work: a beneficent calm and a satisfied hush. Wilson's conversation turned reflective, nostalgic, and went down several decibels. Lavenstein liked to create feelings in others; it was a need of his own.

For Cookie the dinner was not as comforting. She felt confused until she walked outside to fetch more logs. She listened to the soft murmur of the men inside. She leaned against the rough siding of the house. This was something she wanted, the house holding a glow that only food and friends made. But something was missing. Was it telling Coyne about her baby? No, it isn't the baby, Gogarty, and I'll tell you the dark secrets over drams of Black Bush sometime; the door is open and it won't lock again. It's not the baby but the family. My family that I never had is falling to pieces. Benjy: troubled, screwed up, gone. Wilfred: what's left of

153

Pete, after me, and not here for long, and that by a hair. Willard: gone. Lavenstein? Only a question, there. She wanted the roundness of a family, the roundness that meets back on itself. The house was good, the cold roughness of it against her cheek. The glow was good. She wanted more. Among other things, a drink.

When she came in, the table was cleared and Coyne had his yellow pads laid out. He was writing on one as Charlie Bering talked: ". . . only moderately difficult. We didn't try to penetrate any high-security banks but went for peripherals and for an overall pattern. We tried some wild cards—Library of Congress stack permits, traffic tickets, season passes to Redskins games, that sort of thing. We did score on one of the wild cards: Allen Carrol, the dark-haired fellow, has a season ticket for the Washington Symphony. Now we went mainstream. Pay dirt for Marine Corps records: both Carrol and Mark Hunt were career Marine officers, Annapolis trade school boys, two tours, service in Lebanon, intelligence, liaison to joint chiefs, bright boys. They resign their commissions within a month of each other, though there is no indication of a connection before that. Now we get somewhere. Wilson?"

"We get somewhere indeed, Charles. We get to that infamous den of ultraconservative thinkers—the oxymoron of the evening—the Potomack Institute for Democratic Process. Both of our intelligence types show up on the computer, with parking permissions for their building. Both turn up with Avis cards made out to PIDPro, plus AmEx and Visa. We have conservative, trained, bright young men. So far we've described half the squash players at the Capitol Y.

"But stay, my lords and lady. These two conservatively dressed, conservatively styled, conservatively shaped jaspers show up with enough firepower to sink the Anacortes ferry. And the firepower is Company."

154

"I think so," said Coyne. He opened the case to the .50 caliber sniper rifle.

"I know so now, sport," Wilson replied jauntily. "I ran it through a pal at the Smithsonian, a gun wonk named Holiday. These birds are Company or Company companions."

"Companions?" Vern asked.

"Deep boys. Boys that work on things unnoticed by congressional oversight committees."

"Like what, dammit? How does all this fit with Ben? These guys are into drugs? What did you find out about the dentists, Wilson?"

"Charlie ran down some interesting figures on these guys."

"Yeah, well, they're interesting, but what do they mean? We've got major amounts of money coming into their accounts on a regular basis and going out to Caribbean banks on another schedule. They have it all down as 'investment losses,' but when you look at it over a long period, there's a pattern to it and the amounts are the same."

"Back to confusion," Vern said.

Coyne spread out his pads. "Where is the real pattern? We've got Benjy. We've got three, maybe four groups trying to get Benjy. Here are the dentists; they hired me to negotiate. Here is the Mafia, and we assume that Lavenstein's kid was a small-time mafioso making his bones. Here is the government, or some arm of the government, legitimate or illegitimate. Possibility four"—he marked another pad— "federal narcotics agents trying to turn Benjy. Where's the pattern?"

"It's there somewhere," Wilson said. "There on the table."

"But who took Benjy?" Cookie asked.

"Whoever took Benjy hit Wilfred and killed Willard," Coyne said.

Vern leaned forward on his elbows. "And"—he tapped the

155

table with his finger—"and searched the house. Who searched the house and why? Why search the house when they've got Benjy?"

Coyne took Benjy's pad and slid it back and forth slowly, thinking. "And why search the house the way they searched it?"

"Maybe they didn't have time to do it right," Lavenstein said, putting down a bottle of Jack Daniel's and a tray of liqueurs.

"No, they searched for something big. Something they needed in addition to Benjy. Something they knew about."

"But how did they sneak up on Willard?" Cookie asked. "And what could it have been? Benjy took everything he brought with him up to Wilfred's; I packed it all into the saddlebag myself. There was nothing here that wasn't there. Sure as hell nothing big."

Lavenstein tossed Benjy's blue pack on the table, and the half-dozen remaining potatoes rolled out. "The pack," he said.

Charlie Bering's swift fingers dismantled the old Kelty pack. Coyne went through the packsack and the shoulder pads; nothing. Charlie took off the bottom plugs and found it.

"What have we got?" Vern asked.

"Vern." Wilson was spreading the rolled tube out and pegging the corners with bottles. "We've got a section of aerochart marked with the crash site and the route, but look at this: radar installations, refueling stops, times, altitudes. And the route goes below Mexico. Down around Belize."

"God, I hate this," Vern said.

"Wait a minute." Charlie was pulling something else out of the tube, with a skewer from the kitchen. It was wrapped in bubble plastic and taped.

"Come on, Charlie," Wilson said.

"I can do it myself," he replied.

About three inches long, half an inch wide, with golden

spider legs. "It's a chip," said Charlie. "Have you got a hand lens?"

Lavenstein picked it up and examined it under a lens he used for rocks. He shook his head and looked again.

"Well," asked Coyne, "what is it?"

"It's a very high-tech chip," Lavenstein said, "the kind you're not supposed to take out of the country without approval from the State Department. Surely not to Central America. It's the kind of chip you could use to reprogram your fighters for standoff missile warfare, your tanks for fire control, your radar for target guidance. You could do a lot with these, depending on what they're programmed for."

"Could you find out what it's programmed for?" Cookie asked Charlie.

"I don't think he'd want to," Lavenstein replied for him.

"We've got a pattern," Coyne said. "We've got money coming to a laundering service in Charleston, West Virginia, moving in and out from intelligence funds to banks in the Virgins or the Caribbean somewhere. We've got export of high-technology weaponry to a right-wing government in Central America financed by the laundered money. Does the State Department know about this?"

Vern pointed to the sniper rifle. "I think this thing is to keep the State Department from finding out."

"So the dentists are investing only as a cover for this operation?"

"I don't know. They may be investing legitimately too, but they're primarily investing in an overambitious exercise of the Monroe Doctrine."

"Where does the Mafia come in?" Cookie asked.

"Suppose," Coyne said, thoughtfully, "that the deep cover for the operation is a drug-running scheme, except they're running chips. The operation could be closed down at any time, and they could pull any operatives out under federal witness cover.

"The mob knows about any shipments of drugs, or rumors of them. Either they know about the government connection and are trying to take over the route, or they don't know about it and are trying to muscle out the competition of unknown newcomers."

"Does Benjy know about the government connection?" Cookie asked.

"He'd have to. Not enough dope to make a respectable run. Maybe not even any."

"And who chased Benjy's plane?"

"Mob, federales, backup plane from these guys, federal narcs, legit intelligence—could be anyone. Could be no one."

"What?"

"Benjy could have gone into business for himself."

"What now?" Vern asked. "I can hold those two hotshots, Carrol and Hunt, in the hospital for, maybe, two days if the paperwork slows up."

"We've got two jobs, as I see it. Job one, to get Benjy back safe."

"Then kick the shit out of him," Vern said.

"I'll help you," Coyne replied. "Job two, to give everything we've got to the congressional intelligence oversight committee; that will defuse any further harassment. We will be only a minor annoyance to these people."

"How about you, Mr. Coyne?" Vern asked. "How will you be paid?"

"By check, I assume. I have carried out my end of the contract and I will insist"—he stressed the sibilance—"that my fee and expenses be met to the letter. I think, incidentally, that Mr. Bering's findings should aid in a quick payment."

"Benjy, Benjy," Cookie broke in. "How do we get Benjy back?"

158

"The bag," Vern said.

"The blue bag," Coyne repeated, "reassembled. Let's let them see it. They will offer something for its return, like the sportive infant Benjy. How can we arrange it subtly?"

"The funeral," Cookie said. "I'll bring it to Willard's funeral, Saturday, full of pussy willows. Willard's favorite."

CHAPTER TWENTY-TWO

A tear in the clouds opened a sudden light on the cemetery. Against the untorn overcast beyond, Gogarty's vestments were so white that they seemed blurred at the edges. The red-and-purple cross on his breast glowed fervently, and Willard's silver-belly Stetson with the snakeskin band stood out against the dark wood of the coffin. Gogarty's voice went on, unchanged by the light: "The Lord giveth, and the Lord taketh away . . ."

Bert turned to Cookie and murmured, the words coming in a sweet haze of bourbon, "Now if that ain't a square deal, I'll kiss your ass."

Cookie giggled. The ladies near them, the ladies of a certain age who attend all funerals in Cle Elum, looked disapprovingly at them. She smiled back, graciously. It was not a wholly sad occasion; they were celebrating, after all, the spirit of a good friend and a good mechanic and a passable poker player and a good hand. His life was as much the subject, here, as his death, and Willard simply hadn't led a dour life.

Her pussy willows had bloomed for Willard, a gift. A ragged, bright fountain of them sprayed out of Benjy's blue backpack, which was half hidden by other flowers. Just beyond Gogarty and the flowers, a haydriver tipped a pint hip bottle to his mouth surreptitiously in the heads-down gather-

161

ing. Seeing that Cookie had discovered him, he grinned sheepishly. She smiled back. Three handsomely dressed, well-coiffed women stood tearfully among the rear rows of the mourners. Cookie believed that one of them was Mamie herself. Cle Elum was here; not every citizen but parts of the town—waitresses from the coffee shop, haydrivers, feed-store men, plumbers—and they shared their loss in the way John Donne talked about losing a promontory or a part of the main. Unlike Donne's sermon, they were an island, the island of a small town in a chink between mountains. They were the less for their loss.

Gogarty finished, more moved than the crowd because he was not mountain-born, Western-bred, and the principle here was that you shook your head, swore, and went on. Later, plowing or herding or digging a well, you thought about it. The forms that grief took in the East were uncomfortable here, though the emotions were the same. Spread out, per-haps. These people were less hampered by small doses over a longer time, Cookie thought, wondering if her own emo-tions were changing, deepening, coming in bigger pieces. Cookie stepped to the coffin and took the hat. The funeral home's clockwork coffin hoist whirred softly and performed its little contribution to drama; the coffin sank into the Cle Elum earth, leaving the apron of Astroturf around its grave. Well, Willard, that Cub will never run the same.

Cookie was retrieving the backpack and its mass of pussy willows, when one of the well-turned-out women approached her. "You are Ms. Culler, I believe?" A low voice with honey and magnolia in it, and tears.

"Yes," Cookie replied, just managing to shake one of the white-gloved hands by balancing the backpack on her knee.

"I am Mamie Tate," she said, retaining Cookie's hand in her own, backpack still balanced. "From Ellensburg?"

"Yes, Ms. Tate."

"Mrs. Tate. Mamie," she said as if she said it often, looking

162

not at Cookie but at the grave, beginning to cry again. "That man"—she pointed with the other white glove, the one not attached to Cookie—"that man was a gentle man with a nobleness of spirit."

Cookie managed to put the pussy willows and the backpack down, thinking that a southern accent gave the speaker wonderful latitude to use words like "nobleness" and "spirit." "He was a good man," she replied, wondering once again why the terseness of cowboy emotion disturbed her more and more.

Mamie now took both of Cookie's hands in hers, holding with more strength than one would expect of a magnolia blossom. "Dear, you were his family, you know. Willard often visited our little ranch and spoke of you as warmly, as respectfully, and as lovingly—oh, there was loving in that man—as if you were his sister or his daughter. He . . ." She faltered here, and Cookie was moved to leave her hands and put her arms around Mamie. Mamie accepted it for a polite moment and then straightened, trying to regain herself. "Darlin'," she said, with a new voice, a woman-to-woman, let's-have-done-with-this-crying-jag-because-I-need-a-drink voice, "I feel I know you a little, because of poor Willard, and that man always made me laugh, and he was always polite and sweet to me. Brought flowers. Every damn time. How do you find a man like that up here on this cold damn plain? You listen to Mamie, honey: You find yourself someone who remembers little things. You're good people, Ms. Culler—"

"Cookie."

"Well, honey, here. Here's my card with the number right there on it. You take a little time for yourself and come out to our ranch and sit down for an afternoon with the girls and me. Don't worry, now, some real nice Ellensburg ladies like to stop by and just talk. It's like a sorority house, or at least that's what Belinda over there says, who went to Ohio State University and knows. Really, I'd be pleased to see you."

163

"Mamie Tate, you can expect me. I could use some girl talk after these horses and the men who work them. Now we're going down to Mr. McGregor's for a little something after. Father Gogarty says it's the only thing. Will you and your friends join us?"

"That's sweet of you, darlin', but we've got to get back to the ranch." She looked at her watch, a small gold pendant at her collar. "Lord, right quick. You remember, now. You come see Mamie."

"Yes, ma'am," Cookie said, using the respectful title for an elder, though Mamie was only eight or ten years older. She was a handsome woman, but Cookie felt like a little girl with her.

Gogarty had insisted. "Who, I ask you, is the expert on suffering, dying, grieving, sighing? And I answer, the Irish and the Catholic clergy. Step back and learn. Besides that, Gogarty's buying." That settled it.

There was a general squealing of snow tires on dry pavement as a dozen pickups and four-bys were parked at Mr. McGregor's. They filled the bar, noisy but saying little at first. Tom put a handful of red quarters in the jukebox, and the atmosphere relaxed. Cookie, feeling a little out of place in her long skirt and silk blouse, put Willard's hat and boots on the bar, with the backpack fountain of pussy willow blooms. Tom took orders for shooters, drafts, Wild Turkey neat, Lites, a cold Stolichnaya for Lavenstein, Black Bush double for the good father, Jack Daniel's straight for Cookie, and a club soda. Gogarty used his pulpit voice to bray out a Celtic toast over Dolly Parton, and the bar answered with their own replies: "Blood," "Right straight," "Bet your ass," and downed them.

Charlie Bering, usually dressed in a ragged turtleneck, appeared in a blue three-piece suit, looking scholarly and reminding Cookie that he had been a lawyer before Wilson subverted him to the archaeology of greed in corporate

America. Wilson wore a crooked grin and a Harris tweed jacket, already a trifle drunk before the funeral. "Gogarty," he said, "how will a poor priest pay for this expense of liquor? Is the indulgence-selling business coming back, or do you run a small business in contraceptives on the side?"

"I can't understand it, Wilson," Gogarty said sweetly. "God always speaks highly of you."

Vern came in quietly, looking his official best in his pearl-gray hat, his gray pressed uniform, and his black boots. He had been called away from the service by one of the Bellew boys. "Tom," he said, "you got a cup of coffee back there?"

Coyne raised one eyebrow, questioning.

"Seems those two fellas managed to make bail very quickly. Also seems that there were two groups, of two fellas each, watching the service today with spotting scopes and bird glasses. Must be mighty interesting to them, funerals around here."

Coyne sipped his club soda, brow bunched, thinking. "Two groups," he said at last. "Two. I would say that team two was sent with the same purpose as team one. Redundancy."

"And there may be another set of equipment," Lavenstein said. Cookie rubbed against him, needing some reassurance, but Nathan lapsed back into his famous concentration. She could feel Lavenstein's anger at the situation. But she could feel his fear of living too close with it.

"What will they try?"

"Nothing, maybe," Coyne said. "They've seen the back-pack and they'll get in touch with us to make a deal."

"What's our deal?" Cookie asked. "We give them the back-pack and the map and the chip in return for Benjy. We don't have any leverage then. What's to prevent them from killing us?"

"Once they have the backpack, they don't have to kill us, and we make it clear that all the information on the map and

165

the chip will be sent to ten liberal congressmen if one of us is harmed."

"But aren't we playing their game? Aren't we saying it's okay to do what they've done?"

"Like he said," Vern said, "we send the stuff to the committee on intelligence anyway, right?"

"Right," Coyne said.

"How long will it take them to call? How long till we get Benjy back and this thing out of our laps? When can we go back to living?"

"Not long now. Tonight, tomorrow?" Vern said.

"Tonight, if it's acceptable, I'd like to come with you to the ranch," Coyne said. "Look after the backpack. Make sure everything's quiet."

"Come ahead." Lavenstein was relieved.

" 'At's right, Nathan." Vern sipped his coffee. "You can only throw a skillet so far."

P.J. Hambling limped up to the group on his cast. He took off his high-roller hat. "Cooks," he said, "I'm sorry about old Willard. He was a top hand in my book."

Cookie leaned across and kissed his cheek. "Thanks, P.J. Dead right."

P.J. turned to Coyne and extended his hand, wordless but saying much with his eyes. Coyne took his hand and shook it. P.J. raised his glass and Coyne his. They clinked their rims solemnly, Wild Turkey and club soda.

Cookie walked to Gogarty and nestled in under his arm. He was singing a sad Irish song about old times are going, old ways are changing, your traveling days will soon be over. He felt good and she liked his voice, the way he could sing loud with people looking at him, as if it were a natural thing to do, to show what your heart was feeling. She looked down, listening, seeing his black trousers against her long blue skirt, feeling her silk blouse smooth around her shoulders. She thought it might be easier, being a man.

CHAPTER TWENTY-THREE

Pulling her pleasure out of him, Cookie was riding Nathan, on the floor, in front of the dying fire. The glow of the coals reddened each corner, each curve, the hairs of Nathan's chest, as he lay on his back beneath her. But Cookie's eyes were closed as she rode in slow motion, holding his hips with her knees as she rose up and brought his stiffness all along her inner lips, slowly, feeling the bulb of him widen her, perilously close to springing out of her warmth when she would sink back against his thighs, feeling him penetrate and fill her. She swirled her hips against the rod of his shaft in her before she began the slow rise again. She knew how well she did this. Knew how she looked above him, swaying breasts and flexing tummy. Other times she had cruelly, happily ridden him to her will, bringing him toward and away from his orgasm, leaning forward to trace runes of mutual sensation on his chest with her nipples, managing him the way she rode Red through a barrel race. Her will, her pleasure, was the best pleasure she could bring to him. Not now. She was lost in another image, remembering: A little drunk, she had stopped at Vern's and Darlene's, to wake them up and have a drink, no one in the living room through the window but lights on, a soft noise in the backyard, and through the wet grass she walked around the side yard, through the opening in the bushes, to the corner of the house, stopped, and watched Vern and Darlene make love on lawn furniture cushions, watched how they clung, how Darlene cried out his name, begged, demanded, saw Vern's pleasure on her face, hers on his, watched as she began to finger herself, saw their clumsy, homey, tender intimacy, bringing herself to a solitary peak even as she saw the power of their loving, saw the stem and root strength of it expressed in their sex as a flower's delicacy expresses its plant's bond with the soil.

But she had lost the edge of her own concentration now, though she continued to rock against Nathan. She pulled herself away, clasping him even as she left. She crouched and made a long stroke up his body, letting him feel her breasts find the terrain of him, making sure that one nipple lodged for a moment in the hollow of his eye, feeling the texture of her pubis against his soft belly. She brought the center of her sensation up to his mouth and knelt over his head, letting his mouth work at her, clasping her own breasts, feeling his hands knead her buttocks. She thought of Nathan's skill, of the depth Vern and Darlene shared, of Nathan's control, his manipulation, of the distance between them even now as she neared her peak, opening her eyes and seeing herself and Nathan and the room mirrored in the glass frame over a photo of her father.

Coyne was sleeping in the guest room, where the rifle and tack racks made one wall. He heard something, movement, and rose with his Browning. He opened the door a crack. His eyes were keen to the dark, the glow of the subsiding fire seemed bright, and the bodies of Nathan and Cookie, as they made love, as Cookie climbed up on Nathan and knelt over his head, were bright, painted in darks and lights. She swayed and quivered, small sounds coming from her, from Nathan. Coyne envied Nathan as he watched. At that moment Cookie was envying Coyne's lady.

* * *

Early morning. Coyne's eyes opened; he swept the room with his eyes, interrogated his senses, listened. Why had he awakened? His watch gave five fifty-five. He rolled off his bed to one side, taking his automatic from beneath the pillow. Across the floor to the door. What had awakened him?

Standing to one side, he opened his door. Nothing. He stepped into the hall in his shorts, pistol held in both hands ahead of him. Nothing. He came up the hall to Cookie's door. With one hand he pushed the door open. Cookie stood behind it, naked, with her .41 leveled at him. "You ought to lose some weight," she said. "You make the floorboards creak when you sneak around. And you shouldn't watch people fucking." She had seen him in the reflection. The thought of being watched had sent her over the edge. Still, she had to chide him.

"What woke you?" he asked, unconcerned about his voyeurism for a moment.

"I don't know."

"Find out." He motioned to one side of the hall and he took the other. They moved together, two guns ahead of them, into the living room. Only two things were changed: the front door was slightly ajar, and the backpack was gone.

"Damn!" Coyne said.

"How in hell did they pick the damn dead-bolt lock?" Cookie asked. She turned back to her room and started to pull on her clothes.

"Lavenstein, get up, for Christ's sake. Someone's walked right in here and taken the damn backpack."

Lavenstein pulled on his own clothes and dialed Vern's number. "Hey? Nathan Lavenstein here. Get Vern on his radio and tell him and the Bellew boys to close down the road outside Hidden Valley Ranch. Tell him the item is gone. That's right: The item is gone. Tell him to give a call. Thanks."

Cookie was pulling on her boots as she hopped down the

hall. Coyne was dressed. He said, "Whoever it is, they're on foot, and they're headed for the other side of the ridge. They can't have more than ten minutes lead."

"I can saddle up and catch them in five or ten minutes. They couldn't make it to the road."

"Wait," he said, pulling on his own walking boots. "I've got to think a minute."

"That's a big damn lock. Supposed to be pick-proof," Cookie said. Coyne looked at her levelly, telling her to think about something she didn't want to.

Lavenstein appeared, rumpled and testy in his anxiety. "How did they get in? It takes more noise to pick a lock and search a room you don't know. How did this all happen?"

Coyne was right. She didn't want to think about the possibility that forced itself on her with sad, increasing insistency.

Coyne retrieved a bag from the tack room. He brought out one of the Heckler & Koch submachine pistols. He offered it to Lavenstein. "Do you know how to use one of these things?"

"No."

"Okay, there's a pump shotgun in there. You can handle that? Good. Load it with something larger than birdshot."

"Lower-right-hand drawer, red shells," Cookie said, coming out with her saddle Winchester and her .41 holster.

Coyne was assembling the .50 caliber sniper's rifle. "We might need a long shot across the valley," he said.

Cookie snapped the strap across her .41 in the holster and started for the door. "I'll mount up," she said.

"Wait—" Coyne shouted, but Lavenstein had opened the front door, and the burst of automatic fire was almost simultaneous. He spun back into the room over a table and a lamp and there was blood on them when they hit the floor. Lavenstein arched, whimpered, and managed to say, "Shit."

Coyne closed the door with a broomstick from the kitchen.

There was no more fire from outside.

"Shit, shit, shit . . ." Lavenstein was at least alive, hurting.

Coyne rolled him over slowly, face moving with concern. "Get me a sheet," he ordered. He left Nathan for a moment, to look out one window, then another, then he was back at Nathan's side, cutting away his shirt and trousers down one side with a black-handled sheath knife that had appeared from somewhere near his boot. "Three hits: thigh, side, and right through a rib. I think you're going to be okay. Clean, except for this rib; you've got some bone stuff around there." Lavenstein shouted as Coyne felt the wound. He tore and folded the sheet, binding the pads against Nathan.

Cookie looked out a window and ducked down. The window disintegrated and the glass covering a map on the far wall exploded. "Damn! Do something! Do something, Coyne!"

"Not yet." Coyne stayed low and scuttled to the kitchen. He drew a mug of water and poured some sugar, some salt in it, and then baking soda from beside the stove. "Here," he said to Nathan. "Drink as much of this as you can. Cookie, dial Vern."

She dialed. "Hello. Tell Vern that there are shots fired at Hidden Valley Ranch. Yes, we've got one injury. Tell him it's Nathan." She hung up and looked expectantly at Coyne.

"Binoculars," he said. "Stay low."

She handed him the little Minoltas she kept in her saddlebag. He looked at the shots in the wall and at the window, trying to construct the angles. Then he crawled back from the window and rose in a crouch, scanning with the little glasses. "That little house, the yellowish one beside the tractor shed—what's in it?"

"A harrow, a disk, some grain."

He caught a flash of something from the door. "And someone trying to kill us."

Cookie looked at Nathan, sweating on the floor, face

171

screwed into pain. "Just a minute," she said. She scuttled down the hall, and he heard the back door open. She came back and handed Coyne the red tubes. "How far can you throw one of these sonsofbitches?" The blasting gelatin. "There are eight sticks left. If you can get one of these out in front of that shed, I can hit it with the rifle."

"Are you sure?"

She was looking behind her at Nathan. "You watch me, Boston."

"I'll go out the side door and toss them. You put three or four rounds into the shed to keep his head down while I'm out there. Ready?"

She turned back to him. Her face was set hard. "Go," she said.

He stood up beside the door, arranging two sticks of the gelatin in his belt where he could get at them. One stick was in his hand. He unlocked the door, put his hand on the knob, and nodded to her.

Three rounds, spaced by two or three seconds, all in the shed door. It gave time for Coyne to step out onto the porch and throw twice, as if he were tossing sticks for a yellow Lab to retrieve, watch them turn in the air, see that the second landed close, three yards, to the shed. He was back inside, dropping the remaining stick and checking his Browning.

More glass flying, curtains punched in, as Cookie's fire stopped. Coyne nodded at her. "See it?" She looked up, nodded. "How long will you need?"

"Can you hold him down for three or four seconds?"

"Try," said Coyne, getting set. "Ready?" And to her nod he said, "Now."

Coyne rose with his Browning in both hands and fired on the shed, two rounds, four, six, groups of two, and didn't hear Cookie's rifle or even the explosion of the blasting gelatin. He had only the sense of an enormous shock, and his concentration was spent in ducking to the side and down as splinters and dust and gravel showered through the ruined windows.

But Coyne was out the door. Cookie watched, picking herself up again, and saw the fat man moving fast from the porch toward the tractor shed, weaving, low, a shadow in the thinning dust.

She waited.

The wind up the valley of the Souk blew away the dust, and she saw Coyne standing, looking down. Cookie couldn't see Yale, darkened, impaled on four or five tines of the harrow. She watched Coyne drop the magazine of his automatic into his hand and reload it from his pocket, like a man contemplatively charging his pipe with tobacco.

She called out from the window. "Is he down?"

Coyne added a 9mm cartridge to the magazine and simply nodded.

Lavenstein was beginning to bitch in Yiddish, Russian, German, and French. "I've got to get him," she explained, as if Nathan could understand her through his pain and interpret what she really meant. "I've got to go."

In the yard she met Coyne.

"Let's go get him," he said.

"Why not just let him go?" She was pleading. For Benjy. They both knew now that it was Benjy who had opened the door, with the key that Pete and Cookie and Benjy always hid under the porch or under the geraniums. That it was Benjy who hit Wilfred and escaped on his own. That it was Benjy— or Yale or Princeton, but Benjy with them—who killed Willard.

"We could just let him go, Francis."

"We could. They won't. If we don't get him, they will. They can't afford to have him alive, not after he's run once. They've got what they needed: the map, the chip if they knew he had the chip. They'll take him out now."

173

She hesitated.

"Maybe we can get him to the congressional committee. Maybe we can get him some kind of immunity. Maybe. If we get him now."

She looked into his face, looked hard. There was comfort there for her but none for Benjy. Only she had that now. She broke away and ran for the corral. As she saddled good Red, good solid for Christ's sake carry me this day my wonderful Red, her hands shook.

CHAPTER TWENTY-FOUR

Red was spooked by the blast. He shied at Coyne starting the tractor, but Cookie leaned down and gave his ears a scratch, knowing how she would appreciate a simple comfort herself. "Okay, big fella." Her hands and knees and heels told Red to go. He went.

Cookie galloped to the beginning of the path and looked back as she left the road. Coyne was coming on with the tractor, the sniper's rifle across his knees.

Into the rock garden, suddenly fearful that another of Benjy's masters could be waiting with a gun. They rode. Red shifted his powerful body left and right through the maze, Cookie with him, the two making one graceful hybrid machine, and they broke out onto the north side.

Below her she saw Benjy, a small figure running across the bridge with the blue pack toward her pickup, the one he had stolen. Benjy.

Down through the trees, across the open grazing, then, giving Red her heels and a flick with the end of her reins, they jumped the fence. Red was into it now. He took her at a gallop into the creek, with a broad, brown spray of creek water, across, up the bank, and over the road. They had cut Benjy off. Red kept up with the pickup on this turning, soft surface. They were right abreast of the cab.

175

"Benjy! Benjy, stop! Come back, honey; they'll kill you! They can't let you live, Benjy! They'll kill you! God's sake, Benjy, stop!" His face was panicked, the same face he wore when he had broken a china figure of their mother's, one he wasn't to touch: a thick rage of shame and fear and dangerous anger. He looked at the road, at Cookie pleading, at the road, at Cookie; face twitching, he began to shout, a wordless, hopeless, furious lament. He pulled a machine pistol up from the seat beside him and fired a burst into Panama Red's neck.

Cookie and Red went down. Cookie sprawled in the gravel of the road and the dust of the retreating pickup. She rolled over, drew the .41, and rolled flat again. Holding the revolver in both hands, she aimed at the pickup's tire. One shot, dust spurted a foot left. On the second shot she blew the tire. The pickup slewed right and skidded into the ditch.

Still flat, Cookie looked back at Red. The big horse was not struggling, but his eyes were white-rimmed and he was breathing heavily, painfully.

Benjy got out of the pickup with his backpack and his machine pistol.

"Benjy!" Cookie called to him. She saw him hesitate.

A small explosion blew out the windshield and the right side window of the pickup. Benjy was paralyzed with the panic of decision: which way to run? The report of a rifle reached them from a line of trees near the highway.

"Get away from the truck, Benjy! Get away!" she shouted, waving him frantically toward the ditch. He turned toward Cookie and made what may have been a step at the moment the gas tank exploded beside him.

A pillar of sooty flame rose after the fire blossom, and the deep boom echoed from the ridge. The wind was calm, the day was hazy but bright. Cookie lay in the gravel, sobbing,

176

hearing Red wheeze, closing her eyes tight enough to make it all go away.

But it didn't. And the noises from Red were getting worse. She rolled onto her side and pushed herself up with difficulty. She limped back to him. "God damn it, Red," she sobbed, "you dumb sonofabitch. You went and did everything I damn told you to do. And look—look at you." Panama Red, Red the uncomplaining, Red the steady. She pulled back the hammer of her Smith & Wesson .41 magnum and shot the only creature in the world she loved as much as Pete. "So long, partner," she started to say but didn't finish it. She sat down, instead, beside the big red horse.

She didn't hear it at first, the helicopter lifting from the line of trees near the highway, so it was almost on her when she turned toward it. It wasn't the medevac copter. It was coming low, directly toward her. She looked around: open grazing land. The helicopter came on. She scuttled to Red and lay behind him with her .41 propped on him, like a cavalry trooper in a Remington painting. "No, no, no, stop it all," she cried.

The helicopter thudded across her, its shadow passing, and machine gun fire stitched the road around her. Not hit, not this time, you bastards. She fired once at it as it banked over the bridge for another run at her. Cookie pulled herself awkwardly across Red to be on the side away from them, wondering what she would do when they hovered over her to finish the job. Come on and try it, you bastards. Come on over here. But they never did.

As the helicopter pirouetted to a stop in preparation for its run, an explosion formed around its fuselage, high and aft. The helicopter began to turn, slowly at first, and then it blew itself to ragged pieces, which fell, seemingly slowly, into the creek. The untidy pile burned, and little explosions punctuated the roar of its fire.

177

Cookie made it to her feet. She could just see Coyne standing at the entrance to the rock garden, with the sniper's rifle. She waved to show him that she was okay. She looked around her. She knew that she was not okay. She sat down in the road beside Red and continued to cry.

CHAPTER TWENTY-FIVE

Bert and Wilfred were arguing about pickups. Bert was sitting in the driver's seat of a new Dodge with HIDDEN VALLEY RANCH lettered on its doors. He was being reasonable and logical and patient. Willard had missed his chance to kill Bert, but Wilfred would not. Wilfred was telling him the several kinds of an ignorant horse's ass he was, about pickups and all other subjects. Bert liked Wilfred. Somehow, the respect and attention paid him by a patently crazy sonofabitch drove Wilfred into a frenzy. They were a great pair. Their days were never dull.

Spring was firmly in place. The wildflowers were sprayed over the grazing land, and the air was easy on the skin. It was early morning, and the light was magic on the rolling land. The road to Cle Elum was empty. Beside the new pickup stood Cookie, Francis Fulton Xavier Coyne, and Popcorn.

Cookie was holding the reins, trying several plait knots for the ends. "Well, I can't go to the damned plane with you, Francis. Shit, if I did that I might miss you. Know that?"

He nodded, watching her with a genuinely pleasant smile.

"I'm glad Vern's going over, though. Keep you company. Don't talk dirty about me or anything." She tried another knot.

He shook his head, watching her.

"You think that whole thing's wrapped up for us?"

Coyne cleared his throat, as if changing to business had affected it. "I think that once the committee read our statements and looked into them, it was neutralized as far as we're concerned. I think it will go on a long time in Washington, who's going to hang who for what."

"Think we'll be called up to testify or anything?"

"I can't imagine they'll want to hold any kind of hearings on something like this. I think the most liberal members will want this under the table." He looked down the road and saw Vern's four-by far away.

"How about the mob? Do you call it the mob in Boston?"

"I had a talk with an acquaintance in Rhode Island, a Mr. Santore, and an understanding has been reached."

"That's what you're good at, Francis."

"That's what I'm good at."

"Hey. You going to bring that Boston lady and her kids back here to the ranch?"

"I'd like that."

"Plenty of room. I'd like to meet her."

She untied her last knot.

"Will Nathan be here?"

She worked a splash of mud out of the saddle's basket-weave with her fingernail. "I don't think so," she said, looking down the road and seeing Vern's car herself. "He said something about missing good delicatessen, busy schedule, paper held up because of the hospital stay, that sort of thing. No. I think Mr. Lavenstein is hotfooting it." Still, she did not look at him. "Maybe I've gone broody on him or something."

"What will you be up to?"

"Up to? Hell, look around you, Francis. I've got to get the ranch back in shape. Get some new stock. After that, who knows? Take up with the Bellew brothers, maybe. Both of them. At once. Something kinky like that."

"Something steady and warm," he said.

"Sounds like Boston stuff," she said, but she nodded in agreement. She took a deep breath, the kind she might take if she were to jump off a quarry wall into the swimming hole beneath it. "You are a sweet man, Francis. Sweet and gentle. I care about you." She found another mud dab in the saddle.

"Me too," he said. "But . . ."

"Yeah. It's okay. It's nice. Well. There's old Vern. Like I said, don't be talking bad about me, and I mean it about the lady and her whole fucking brood. Get 'em out here in high summer, this summer. I've got some real gentle horses to put 'em on. As for you, Francis, I had a chat with Wallace Beery this morning, and he said to tell you to think about . . . ah . . . losing some pounds if you're coming along."

"I'll think about it."

Coyne reached into the pickup and shook hands with Bert and Wilfred. Cookie mounted.

"Popcorn, you neurotic sonofabitch, settle down. It's only Vern's car. I swear, you're going to get less neurotic, or you're going to be eaten from cans by dogs. You hear me?" She scratched Popcorn's ears. She gave him a little nudge of heel and walked him around. She squinted at the low sun and at the grazing land, looking at the situation. Vern's four-by was pulling up.

"Tell you what, Francis," she called. He turned from the pickup and looked back at her as she gave both heels and the end of the reins to Popcorn. They bolted up the road and she shouted back: "I'll send you a picture of me naked on a bearskin!"

Cookie and Popcorn jumped the fence.